Dear Readers,

I am writing to tell you about how I came to write *Summer Ball*, one of my favorite books. And the true story on this particular story is that it came about because of *you*.

My first book for young readers was called *Travel Team*, about a seventh-grade basketball player named Danny Walker who gets cut from his travel team for being too small. It was about Danny, about his friends Tess and Ty and Will, about heart and friendship and picking yourself up after getting knocked down.

It made readers all over the country cheer.

Later, as I traveled around the country talking about new books, I was amazed at how many questions I still got about *Travel Team*, readers wanting to know whether Danny's team went on to win the national championship of 12-year-old basketball, what had happened to him and his friends. I found out these characters had become as real to readers — it is always the magic of a good book — as they had to me.

I felt I owed everybody the answers to those questions. So I pick up Danny's story two years later. *Summer Ball* is about how Danny, still too small, gets knocked down at a summer basketball camp in Maine and has to pick himself up — with the help of his friends — all over again.

I hope he makes you cheer all over again.

Your friend in books,

Mike Lupica

Mike Lupica

MIKE LUPICA

SUMMER BALL

SCHOLASTIC INC.
New York Toronto London Auckland Sydney
Mexico City New Delhi Hong Kong Buenos Aires

ISBN-13: 978-0-545-10905-5
ISBN-10: 0-545-10905-1

12 11 10 9 8 7 6 5   9 10 11 12 13/0

Printed in the U.S.A.   40

First Scholastic printing, September 2008

Design by Gina DiMassi

This is another book for my wife, Taylor,
and for our children:
Christopher, Alex, Zach and Hannah Grace.
They have, all of them, made me believe
in happy endings.

ACKNOWLEDGMENTS:

My parents, Bene and Lee Lupica.
And my wife's parents, Cecily Stoddard Stranahan and
the late Charles McKelvy. Who have always given so much,
and asked so little in return.

DANNY WALKER SAID TO HIS PARENTS, "YOU KNOW THAT GROWTH spurt you guys have been promising me my whole life? When does that kick in, exactly?"

They were all sitting at the kitchen table having breakfast: Danny, his mom, his dad. Richie and Ali Walker were finally back together, after having been apart for way too much of Danny's life, for reasons he always said he understood but didn't.

None of that mattered to Danny now. The three of them having breakfast like this had become strictly regulation, instead of something that felt like it ought to be a family holiday.

Richie Walker put down his newspaper and said to his wife, "Which growth spurt do you think he's talking about?"

Ali Walker, chin in her hand, frowning at the question, a real Mom pose if there ever was one, said, "It can only be the big one."

"Oh," Richie said, "the *big* one."

"Not to be hurtful," Danny's mom said to his dad, "but it's the growth spurt you never really had, dear. Whatever the nice people listing your height in the programs always had to say about you."

"Came close," he said.

Ali grinned. "Missed it by *that* much."

Now Richie looked at his son. "And despite being the size that I am, I still managed to be All-State at Middletown High, get a scholarship out of here to Syracuse, get to be All-America there and become a lottery pick in the NBA."

"Blah, blah, blah," Danny said.

"Excuse me?" his dad said.

"Kidding."

There was no stopping his dad on this one. It was like he was driving to the basket. You just got out of the way.

"And," Richie Walker said, "though my memory gets pretty fuzzy sometimes, I believe before I did all that, I was the point guard on the Middletown team that won the nationals in travel ball when I was twelve. Like another twelve-year-old I know."

"I get it, Dad," Danny said. "Seriously. I get it, okay? I know this act you and Mom like to do the way I know my *Boy Meets World* reruns."

His best bud, Will Stoddard, had gotten Danny hooked on the show. Will knew more about television shows, old and new, than about any school subject he had ever taken in any grade with any teacher. Danny thought Will secretly wanted to be an actor someday; he might as well get paid for performing, since he'd been doing it his whole life.

Ali said, "I thought *Saved by the Bell* was your fave."

"I go back and forth." Now Danny was the one grinning. He didn't know if other kids liked just sitting around with their parents this way. But he never got tired of it.

"Hello?" Richie said. "I wasn't quite finished."

"Sorry, dear," Ali said.

"Missing my own big growth spurt and never actually growing to the five-ten they always listed me at in those programs also didn't prevent me from getting the girl."

Girls.

It was the absolute, total, last thing on earth he wanted to talk about today. Or think about. Today or ever again, maybe.

One girl in particular, anyway.

"I'm happy for both of you," Danny said. "But, Dad, I know you weren't the smallest kid in every game you ever played. And I am. Sometimes it gets kind of old."

"Yeah, like you're getting old. You just finished the eighth grade, after all. And will be fourteen years old before you know it."

"And just had a losing record for the first time in my life," he said to his dad.

"Horrors!" Ali Walker said. "Six wins and seven losses. Shouldn't we have grounded him for that?"

"Funny, Mom."

"I don't suppose it matters that you were an eighth grader basically playing on a ninth-grade team, and going up against teams that had *all* ninth graders," his dad said.

"You know what your man Coach Parcells always said," Danny said, loving it when he could turn one of his father's sayings around on him. "You are what your record says you are."

"You did fine."

"And we wouldn't have won as many games as we did if Ty hadn't transferred," Danny said.

Ty Ross was his other best bud. Meaning a *guy* bud. And Ty was a lot more than that. In Danny's opinion, he was the best basketball player in town. Of any age. There were a bunch of people who said Ty and Danny were co-best, even though Ty was already a foot taller, but Danny wasn't buying it. He also didn't care what people said—he was just happy to have Ty playing Karl (the Mailman) Malone to his John Stockton, all the way through high school.

Ty had switched from his own travel team to Danny's the year before, mostly so he could play with Danny, and then their team, the Warriors, won the same travel championship Richie Walker's team had once won. At the time, Ty was still going to the Springs School, the public school in town. But he had talked his parents into letting him move over to St. Patrick's, just for one year, so he and Danny didn't have to wait until they got to ninth grade at Middletown High to start playing freshman ball together.

Or maybe they'd even skip freshman ball, now that the new varsity coach at Middletown High, starting next season, was going to be Richie Walker himself. Sometimes Richie hinted that he might have them both go straight to varsity, since most of this year's team had just graduated.

When his dad would drop those hints, Danny would just go along, try to act excited, even though he wondered how he would be able to go up against high school seniors in a few months after nearly getting swallowed whole by the taller ninth-graders this past season.

"Wait till you and Ty are playing for Coach Walker," Richie said now.

"Yeah, Dad," Danny said. "It'll be *sick*."

He knew he'd made a mistake the minute he said it. The way he knew when he'd thrown a dumb pass the *instant* the ball left his hands.

He knew because his mom immediately went into one of her fake coughing fits, saying in a weak voice, "So, so sick."

"Sorry, Mrs. Walker," Danny said in a whiny student's voice.

"You can talk MTV with your friends," she said. "But in here, we sort of try to keep a lid on *sick*, right?"

Danny sighed an I-get-it sigh.

"I gotta grow!" he shouted.

"You will!" his parents shouted back.

"When?" A voice so quiet it seemed to be at the bottom of his bowl.

His parents looked at each other, smiling, and shouted again. "Soon!"

"I'm gonna be smaller than ever when I get up to Maine for the stupid camp," Danny said. "Seriously, Dad. If I'm as small as I am around Middletown, what's going to happen up there?"

"What's happened your whole life," Richie Walker said. "Every single time you've been challenged or gotten knocked down or had to prove yourself all over again, you are *sick*."

"I give up," Ali Walker said.

It was the second Saturday after school had let out. The breakfast plates and bowls had been cleared by the men in the family, a Saturday rule. Danny and his dad were outside now, on the small court at the end of the driveway at 422 Earl Avenue, Richie feeding him the ball as Danny moved around on the outside and shot what passed for his jump shot.

Every time Danny put the ball on his shoulder and launched it the way he had when he was even littler than now, when it was the only way for him to get the ball to the hoop, Richie would yell "stop!" and make him shoot with the proper motion from the same spot, hands in front of him.

"This is the perfect time for you to go to a big-time camp," Richie said. "We've gone over this."

Danny, quoting his dad, said, "You gotta keep taking it to the next level, or you never leave the one you're at."

"I'm not sure that's the way your mom would put it in a sentence," Richie said. "But you know it's true, guy."

"I didn't do so hot at the level I was just at," Danny said. "And we weren't even playing all the best schools around here."

"You're being too hard on yourself," Richie said, then threw him a perfect bounce pass. Danny caught it, did the little step-back move he'd been using since he first started playing, the one that created the space he needed between him and taller defenders, the one that kept him from getting a mouthful of rubber every time he tried to get a shot airborne.

This one he swished, then he kept his right hand in the air, holding the pose.

"In the driveway you can show off," his dad said. "Never on the court."

"Gee, I don't think I've ever heard that one before."

"Let's take a break for a second," Richie said.

All he'd been doing was standing there feeding the ball, yet he looked more tired than Danny. His dad never mentioned it, but he couldn't stand for long periods of time anymore. He'd had two real bad car accidents in his life—the first one ending his NBA career, the second one on an icy road during the travel season last year—and joked that his body now had more spare parts in it than some old pickup truck built from scratch at the junkyard.

His knees were completely shot, he said, swelling up with new sprains all the time. Ali had made him go get an X-ray the day before, wanting to see if there was something more serious going on.

Now his dad groaned and rubbed the side of his right knee and said, "X-ray perfect, knee horrible."

The two of them sat down on the folding chairs they kept on the side of the court, like it was the Walkers' team bench, for one coach and one player.

"Dave DeBusschere told me something once that explains why you need to go to this camp better than I ever could," Richie said. "You know who he was, right?"

"Old Knick," Danny said. "He played on that Knicks team you said played ball as right as any team ever."

"Smartest team ever, even though they're like ancient history now," he said. "Clyde Frazier, Earl (the Pearl) Monroe, Willis Reed, Senator Bill Bradley. They were smarter even than Bird's Celtics or Magic's Lakers. Best passing team ever. All the stuff we think is cool about basketball."

"Soooooo cool," Danny said.

"Anyway, he told me something before a game at Madison Square Garden one night I never forgot. He was running the Knicks then. He said that we all start out just wanting to be the best kid on our block, and some of us get to be that. But as soon as we do, almost like the minute we do, you know what happens, right?"

Somehow Danny just knew. "You find out about a kid on the next block."

He and his dad bumped fists.

"So you find out how you can handle yourself against him. Prove to yourself you can play with *him*. Only, as soon as you do that, you hear about this kid on the other side of town. Then in the next town, somebody hears about you and thinks he can absolutely kick your butt. Now you gotta go play him. Because you just gotta know."

"It sounds like it never ends."

Richie Walker smiled, put his arm around his son.

"Not if you're good enough, it doesn't," he said.

"The first day up there," Danny said, "they're gonna think I'm ten."

"Only until you start dribbling that ball."

His dad left, needing a rest now. Danny stayed out there. It didn't matter where he was or who he was playing with, he was always the last one on the court.

Out there alone, as he had been about a thousand other times in his life. Not shooting now, just keeping the ball on a low dribble, right hand, left hand, through his legs, behind his back, never looking at it, doing his double-crossover, imagining himself as some kind of basketball wizard.

Danny Walker, alone with a basketball, and a secret.

The secret being this:

He was scared.

He was scared even though he'd never come out and admit that to his parents, even though there was a time not very long ago when he and his teammates had felt like the most famous twelve-year-olds in America. Not just scared about going off to basketball camp. Scared that the seventh-grade travel championship that he and the Warriors had won might be the best it ever would be for him in basketball.

Oh, sure, they had gone up against the other best seventh-graders in the country. But even though Danny was the smallest one out there, they were all the same age. Pretty soon, basketball wouldn't work that way. Danny Walker—who wasn't just smart about basketball, who was smart, period—knew that.

Basketball at camp was going to be like *real* ball. His age group wouldn't just be thirteen-year-olds. It went from thirteen through fifteen. If he couldn't handle some of the ninth-grade guards he'd gone up against this year, what was going to happen when he went up against some guy who was getting ready to be a junior in high school?

That was part of Danny's secret.

Here was another:

He wasn't going because he couldn't wait to take on the kid from the next block over, couldn't wait to get to the next level, oh yeah, bring it on. That was the way his dad looked at things. No,

Danny was going because he had to find out for himself if he could cut it once he got in with the *real* big boys.

When he'd gotten cut from travel that time, he knew in his heart that it was because a bunch of adults thought he was too small. And then he'd shown them they were wrong.

Now Danny, as brave as he tried to act in front of his parents and his buds, wasn't sure he could keep showing everybody forever.

This wasn't just about size anymore. It was about his talent and, if he really thought about it, his dreams. Especially the big dream, the one about him someday doing more in basketball than even his dad.

Danny had to *know*.

IT WASN'T JUST ANY SUMMER BASKETBALL CAMP THEY'D FINALLY DE-cided to go to, not by a long shot.

This was Josh Cameron's Right Way Camp, about an hour outside of Portland, Maine, in a town called Cedarville.

Josh Cameron, just two years younger than Richie Walker, was the star point guard of the Boston Celtics, having won more championships with the Celtics than Larry Bird had. He was Danny's second favorite player, after Jason Kidd, and he was always talking about playing basketball "the right way." Right before he'd go out in the next game and show people exactly what he meant by that.

He was listed at 6-2 in the program, which probably made him five inches taller than Danny's dad in real life, not that Richie Walker would ever admit to something like that. What Richie would say about Josh, though, every time the subject came up, was this:

His size had never held him back, either.

And every time he would say that, Danny would think, *Where do I sign up, right now, to be 6-2 someday?*

Where do I sign up to be whatever height, 5-9 or 5-10, that my dad really is?

According to Richie, Josh Cameron had started Right Way with the help of one of his old college teammates about ten years ago. Now it was supposedly on a level with the Five-Star camps that all teenage basketball players had heard about. It had become such a big deal that college scouts would come up to Maine every July and even start looking at seventh and eighth graders they might want to think about recruiting someday.

The "junior" part of the camp, the July part, was limited to kids between the ages of eleven and fifteen. The elevens and twelves went into one league, Danny knew from the brochure; the older kids into another. Later on in the summer, there was a separate camp for elite players about to enter their senior year in high school. But in either session, Right Way was all basketball, all the time—clinics and instruction in the mornings, games in the afternoon and at night. Because of who Josh Cameron was, he got top college coaches to come to Cedarville and every year would get some of the most famous college players in the country to come work as counselors.

Starting next week, Danny and Ty and Will would be going up against the best kids in the country. Until then, Will and Ty seemed to have made it their sworn duty to bust chops on Danny every time he'd even suggest that he'd just rather stay home this summer and hang out.

"I'm the one who should be looking to stay home," Will said now. "You both know I'm not good enough to be going to this camp."

"Sure you are," Danny said, halfway believing it by now. "You're a great shooter and you know it."

"But all I can *do* is shoot," Will said. "The only reason I got in is because your dad made them take me."

Danny grinned. "Maybe he did."

"I *knew* it!" Will said.

"If you don't think you belong, why don't you stay home, then?" Danny said.

"And mow lawns in our neighborhood like my parents want me to?" Will said. "I'd rather miss jump shots for a month."

"In the place known as Will World," Ty said, "I guess that's what passes for a shooter's mentality."

Will ignored Ty and said to Danny, "You're not hacked off because you have to go up to Maine and kick butt, by the way. Oh, no, no, no. You, my friend, are hacked off because you're having trouble with your main *squeeze*."

Meaning Tess Hewitt.

Will looked at Ty for approval, which is what he did when he wasn't looking to Danny for approval after he got off what he considered to be a good line. The three of them were lying in the grass after a couple of hours of made-up shooting drills on the outdoor court at McFeeley, the best in Middletown. "Get it?" Will said. "Maine? Main squeeze? Gimme some love."

Ty lazily raised his right arm, got it close enough to Will that they could give each other high fives.

"Tess is not my main squeeze," Danny said. "And on what planet, by the way, do they still even talk like that?"

"She is, and you know it. *Everybody* knows it."

Louder than he intended, Danny said, "She is not!"

"Which happens to be the problem," Will said, "even if you are too terminally dense to see that."

"If there is a problem," Danny said, "it's her problem, wanting to hang out with him rather than do what she's always done and hang around with us."

Him was Scott Welles. Will called him Scooter, even though nobody else did. He had moved to Middletown halfway through the school year from Tampa, where he'd been about half a tennis prodigy at the Harry Hopman Tennis Academy, a place a lot of famous tennis players had passed through on their way to the pros. But his father was a doctor and had gotten a big offer from the North Shore Medical Center, not too far from Middletown. So the family had moved north and his parents had enrolled Scott for second semester at St. Patrick's.

As soon as he joined the tennis team at St. Patrick's, he proceeded to win every singles and doubles match he played all year.

He also won the occasional mixed doubles match he played with Tess Hewitt, who had taken lessons all winter, really concentrated on tennis for the first time in her life, and turned out to have a better forehand than Maria Sharapova's.

In addition to being the tennis star of the whole county and probably all of Long Island, Scott Welles proved to be one of the smartest kids in their class and looked like he ought to be starring in one of those nighttime shows like *One Tree Hill*.

And he was tall.

Taller than Ty and Will, even.

When Danny walked next to Tess, something that was happening less and less, he still looked like her little brother. When Scott Welles walked next to her, or stood next to her on a tennis court, he looked like a guy in basketball who'd gotten a good mismatch for himself in the low post.

Now that it was summer, the two of them were the best players on the town tennis team at the Middletown Field Club. Danny asked Tess one time near the end of school what had happened to photography and the way she loved to take pictures, and she joked, "You worried that I might get as good at tennis as you are at basketball?"

Town tennis in summer was sort of like travel basketball had been. They had started right in as soon as school let out and had played three or four matches against other towns already. All of a sudden, if Tess wasn't playing a match somewhere, she was practicing.

Mostly with Scott Welles.

Danny hardly saw her at all anymore, unless he happened to ride his bike past the field club or the tennis courts at McFeeley near the back entrance to the park. Every once in a while, Danny would talk to Tess online, but it wasn't every night the way it used to be. And it wasn't as fun, or *funny,* as it used to be. Nothing was the way it used to be when it was just the four of them—Danny, Will, Ty, Tess—when they were the Four Musketeers.

Before Scott Welles had to move to town.

On the grass at McFeeley, the afternoon stretched out in front of them like an open court. It was the kind of afternoon that made Danny wonder sometimes why he wanted to go anywhere this summer. He said, "She'd just rather be with him than with us, is all."

Back to Tess. Whatever kind of conversation they were having lately, somehow it always came back to that.

"I actually think she'd rather be spending more time with *you,*" Ty said.

"Captain Cool on the court," Will said. "Captain Klutz off it."

"What's that mean?"

"It means," Ty said, "that you and Tess used to be able to read each other's minds, and now you can't even talk to each other."

Before Danny could say anything back, to either one of them, Will said, "Dude, can we get *real* serious for a minute?"

Will didn't want to get serious too often. But when he did, you had to pay attention. Danny knew how smart Will was once you got past all his jokes, like you were breaking a full-court press. In school, he got straight As even though he studied about half the time Danny did.

"Talk to me," Danny said.

"You know Tess is just hanging around with Scooter because of tennis," Will said. "When we get back from camp, and for sure by the time we're back in school, the two of you will be as tight as ever."

"You don't know that."

"Yeah, I do."

Nobody said anything. They each had their own ball, and there was a moment when all three balls were being spun toward the sky.

"Okay, now you answer me a serious question," Danny said.

"About Tess or camp, those're the only things we talk about these days. Especially now that you and Tess *aren't* talking."

"Camp," Danny said. "Are you really all that fired up for it?"

Will grinned. "Doesn't matter whether I am or not. You know the only reason I'm going is because you guys are going." He acted like he was talking to both of them now, but Danny really knew he was talking to him. Will had known Danny longer, and better, than he knew Ty, no matter how much they hung with each other now. "If you're there, I'm there," Will said. "I got your back, dude. In everything. Forever. That's the deal."

The only thing you could do when he said something to you like that was bump him some fist. Danny would never tell it to him this way, but the coolest thing about Will Stoddard wasn't the way he made him laugh. It was that Danny already knew he had the best friend he was ever going to have in his life.

"I'm happy you're going with me," Danny said. "And that Ty's going, especially since he could go to any camp he wanted. I just wish I was happier *I* was going."

"C'mon," Will said. "Basketball *always* makes you happy. It's who you are, dude. Your whole life, every single time you need to show somebody new that you have game, you show them. *Big*-time."

"You sound like my father."

"Okay," Will said. "That hurt."

"All I'm *trying* to say," Danny said, "is that it's been a while since I had to go through all that first-day-of-school crap. And don't tell me it's not gonna happen, because you both know it is. We'll be there about ten minutes, and somebody's going to tell me I'm not supposed to be up with the older kids. I just don't need that anymore."

It wasn't the whole truth, the part about him being scared, but it would do for now.

Ty and Will looked at each other, like they didn't know who should go first. Ty said, "You take it."

Will said, "Yeah, nobody's going to have any idea who you are after you've won travel and did all the TV we did. You got to be the most famous twelve-year-old in America for a while."

"We were all famous," Danny said.

Will shook his head.

"They *liked* us," Will said. "They *loved* you." He grinned. "The way Tess does."

"You're a freak," Danny said.

Sometimes Will called the whole thing *Saved by the Ball Handler*— everything that had happened after Danny had gotten cut from the regular seventh-grade travel team in Middletown, the Vikings. Right after that, Richie Walker came back to town and started up another team, one made up mostly of other kids who'd gotten cut, and somehow got them into the Tri-Valley League after a team dropped out.

Things got crazy after that.

Danny became a twelve-year-old player/coach after his dad's car accident. Ty, who'd been playing for the Vikings—a team *his* dad coached—switched teams. The Warriors ended up beating the Vikings in the league championship game on a *sweet* feed from Danny to Ty at the buzzer.

Then they really got on a roll, winning the regionals at Hofstra University, playing their way to North Carolina—the Dean Dome!—for the semis and finals.

They showed the finals, against the travel team from Baltimore, on ESPN2. By then a lot of media from around the country, not just from the New York area, had gotten pretty fired up about the team from Middletown coached by Richie Walker's son, trying to win the same travel title that had put Richie on the map when he was Danny's age.

It didn't seem to hurt the story that Richie Walker's son looked little enough to be ten.

If that

Middletown ended up beating Baltimore in the final game, 48–44. Baltimore was supposed to be better, *lots* better, mostly because of a miniature Allen Iverson playing for them—same hair as number 3 of the 76ers, even a couple of tattoos—named Rasheed Hill. But Danny finally came up with a cool box-and-one defense after Rasheed had torched everybody who tried to cover him for twenty of his team's twenty-four points in the first half.

Rasheed fouled out with three minutes to go, Danny drawing a charge on him. The Warriors were down six points at the time, but from there to the finish, it was the Danny Walker–Ty Ross show in the Dean Dome. Danny kept feeding Ty the ball, or sometimes just running isolation plays for him, and nobody could stop him.

And when it was all in, like they said on the poker shows, nobody could get in front of Danny Walker.

Danny was the one who finally put his team ahead for good with a steal and a layup. Then Ty sealed the deal with a bunch of free throws in the last minute, making them as easily as he did when he gave Danny and Will a good beatdown at McFeeley if the two of them were silly enough to challenge him to a free throw shooting contest.

After that, everything was in fast-forward mode. They did a satellite interview on Regis and Kelly. The whole team got to go to New York City and do a Top 10 list with David Letterman. They even visited the White House. The highlight of their visit, at least as far as Danny was concerned, was Will Stoddard asking the president if he had any game.

When the president had shaken Danny's hand, right before Danny presented him with a Warriors jersey that had the number 1 on the back, the president had said, "You sure are following in your dad's footsteps, aren't you, little guy?"

Danny thought that day, *Man, you can even get little-guyed by the president of the United States.*

It was the beginning of the best year of his life. His dad got back together with his mom. Now his dad had decided to take the coach's job at Middletown, in addition to the weekend college basketball show he was doing for SIRIUS Satellite Radio. And, like the whipped cream on top of a brownie sundae, Ty had done his transfer thing so he could come play with Danny and Will and a lot of the other Warriors who were already attending St. Patrick's.

Basically, Danny Walker had still felt like he was getting carried around on everybody's shoulders.

Then came his varsity season at St. Pat's: six wins, seven losses, too many games when Danny didn't just feel like he got little-guyed by the other team but felt like some ninth grader on that team had made him disappear completely.

On top of that, Scott Welles moved to town.

So more than a year after the biggest win of his life, it didn't take some kind of nuclear scientist to figure out why he was feeling smaller than ever these days.

Will got up, saying to Danny, "You want to go to Subway with Ty and me?"

"Not hungry."

"You pack yet for camp?" Ty said.

"Not yet."

"You want to go see the new Vince Vaughn movie tonight?" Will said. "It's actually PG-13."

"Not in the mood."

"Not, not, not," Will said. "You know you sound like a *knot*head lately, right?"

"Thank you."

"Wait," Will said, getting that look he got when he was sure he had come up with another brilliant idea. "Why don't I call Tess on her cell, tell her why you're moping around like the world-class mope of the universe, and ask her if she can do something to make you less jealous, just till we get to Maine?"

Will wasn't trying to be mean. He wasn't wired that way. There were just times when he knew, and Danny knew, that he just had to push Danny's buttons to get him to lighten up.

Do anything to get a smile out of him, no matter how challenging that seemed sometimes.

Like now.

"You know," Danny said, "one of these days I'm going to figure out a way to out-annoy you."

"It can't be done," Will said.

Then he said he and Ty were going to Subway, and right then, whether Danny wanted to come along or not.

Danny preferred to stay and work a little more on his shot, said he was going to start getting his head right for Right Way now, so he'd be ready for the big boys next week.

"Got to bring my A game," Danny said.

"On the worst day of your life," Ty said quietly, meaning it, "you're an A-minus."

Will said, "You sure you don't want me to talk to Tess?"

"Please go," Danny said, then said something he said to Will all the time: "I'll pay you."

"But you do plan to talk to her before we go, right?"

"Sure," Danny said. "I just don't happen to feel like it right now."

"Well," Will said, "start feeling like it, Sparky. Because here she comes."

3

SHE WAS WEARING A WHITE, COLLARED TENNIS SHIRT AND WHITE TEN-
nis shorts, carrying her racket, hair tied back into a ponytail. There
were hard courts and clay courts at McFeeley, but you could see the
hard courts from the basketball court. Tess must have been playing
on the clay courts, on the other side of the big baseball field.

Probably with Mr. Perfect.

Danny watched her come toward him, happy to see her despite
everything that had been going on—or not going on—but still
thinking, *Man, her legs are longer than I am.*

He heard Will and Ty yell "hey, Tess," as they walked in the
other direction, toward town.

"Hey," she said when she got to Danny.

"Hey."

Maybe he was Captain Klutz when it came to girls. Even this
girl, who could walk around and be better looking than any girl in
Middletown and still hang with the guys like a champ.

She dropped her racket into the grass, next to his big bottle
of blue Gatorade. Danny always liked it better if they were sitting
when they were together, because it made him feel like they were
the same size.

"So," she said, forcing a smile on him, "you guys ready to go?"

"Next Saturday," he said. "Good old JetBlue from JFK to Portland. Then a bus to camp."

"So you decided on the one in Maine."

He hadn't talked to her since they'd made it official, chosen Right Way over a couple others Richie Walker had considered for Danny and the guys.

"We did," he said.

"What town is it in?"

"Cedarville."

For some reason, the name made Tess laugh. Hard. "Cedarville, Maine?" she said.

Danny said, "What's so funny?"

Tess said, "Nothing."

"Something."

"I'll tell you later," she said, like this was just one more inside joke that girls were in on and boys weren't.

They sat there, Danny with his head back now, staring at the clouds moving slowly across a blue, blue sky.

"You must be excited," Tess said.

"I guess."

"You guess?" Tess said, sounding like the old Tess. "You'll be great up there. You haven't gotten to play a real game since the season ended. I know you, Walker. The way you look at things, there's basketball games, and there's killing time."

"That's not true."

"Totally true."

The next thing just came out of him, like a dumb, dumb shot you knew you shouldn't have taken the second you hoisted it up. "Where's Scott? I thought the two of you did everything together these days."

Tess didn't say anything right away, just stared at him until she finally said in this low voice, "Wow."

"I just meant—"

"Pretty clear to me what you meant."

"Maybe it came out wrong."

"You think?"

There was another silence between them then, one that felt as big as McFeeley Park. Ever since they had known each other, from the first grade on, it had been like they could finish each other's sentences. Sometimes, when they were IM-ing at night, they would type almost the exact same thing at the exact same time. But when they were IM-ing each other every night. Before something had come between them.

Or somebody.

Maybe Will was right.

Maybe he was just jealous.

"Danny," Tess said.

She hardly ever used his first name when they were talking, even on the computer. But when she did, she meant it was time for them to get serious.

Danny waited.

"Things shouldn't be this weird between us," she said. "I mean, it is *us,* right?"

Danny had always figured that girls were smarter than boys when it came to understanding most things, figured that the only place where boys had them beat was sports and video games.

But Tess Hewitt was smarter than all of them.

"I don't know what you mean," Danny said, even though he knew exactly what she meant, as usual.

"Yes, you do."

Busted.

He said, "I'm not the one who changed everything."

"You're saying I did?"

"Maybe I am."

"You think this is all because of Scott, don't you?"

"You mean Mr. Perfect."

It came out more sarcastic than he intended.

Another air ball.

"What, you're the only one who's supposed to be great at something?" she said. "I must have missed that chapter in *Danny Walker's Rules for Life.*"

She looked down and said, "In a way, you're the one who stopped hanging around with me."

"What's that supposed to mean?"

"Once Ty started going to St. Patrick's, all of a sudden it had to be the four of us or none of us."

"That's bull."

"No, it isn't."

He spun the ball on his finger again, then slapped it away from him. "No," he said. "Uh-uh. Stuff changed when you started spending all your free time with Mr. Perfect."

Tess shook her head. "It wasn't like that."

"Looked that way from where I was."

He knew he had to get out of this. But it was too late.

"You know what I really think?" Danny said. "If it's this easy for you to stop hanging around with me and start hanging around with somebody else, then maybe we were never really that close friends in the first place."

Tess opened her mouth and closed it, her face redder than ever now.

"Maybe it just made you feel big, hanging around with the little guy," he said.

She kept staring at him, eyes starting to fill up now, these little pink dots suddenly appearing all over her face. Danny was afraid she was going to start crying.

And he had never seen Tess cry.

Not the time her sled hit that tree when they were sledding in the winter at Middletown Golf Club and she'd broken her wrist. Not when Prankster, her first cat, had died. Not when she'd taken that tennis ball in the face a few weeks ago in a school match Danny had forced himself to watch, even if he hadn't told Tess he was going to be there.

He wanted to stop this now, in the worst way. The first time she cried in front of him, he didn't want it to be because of him.

He just didn't know how.

Neither did Tess. Who didn't cry, as close as she'd come, who just kept staring at him as she bent over to pick up her racket, her hand shaking a little.

He sat where he was, really not wanting to stand next to her today.

She left without a word, just turned and walked straight across the court. Danny suddenly wanted to yell for her to come back, tell her he was sorry for acting like a jerk. But just as he got up to do that, he saw Scott Welles, Mr. Perfect in his own perfect tennis clothes, looking like he hadn't even played yet, not even sweating, coming from the direction of the clay courts.

Tess stopped halfway between them.

Right before Scott got to her, she quickly turned around, just for a second, the sad look still on her face. Then Scott Welles took her racket from her, and the two of them walked through the main arch at McFeeley Park, like they were walking right out of Danny's summer.

As soon as they were gone, Danny collected his basketball, went back out on the court. It was usually his favorite thing, having a court like this all to himself. Just not today. Today, he stood on the half-court line and bounced the ball so hard, with both hands, it was like he was trying to put a meteor-size hole in it.

Danny dribbled the ball then, like a madman, up and down the court, putting it between his legs, behind his back, using his old double-crossover move, dribbling as well—almost—with his left hand as with his right.

He did this all nonstop, going up and back like there was a coach out there yelling at him to do it, and finally pulled up at the pond end of the court and drained a twenty-footer.

Nothing but net.

Was he some kind of moron, acting like he didn't want to get to camp, get away from here?

Get away from her?

Man, all of a sudden he couldn't wait to get to Maine. Maybe this is what he needed, to get mad about something the way he had gotten mad when he first got cut from travel.

Behind him now, he heard Will say, "Just for the record, are you winning the game against the imaginary player, or losing it?"

They must have wolfed their sandwiches.

Ty said, "Maybe he's replaying the game against Baltimore. Possession by possession."

"Or *maybe*," Will said, "he's going one-on-one with Scooter Welles," before he quickly covered up and added, "Please don't hurt me."

Danny said something his dad liked to say to him. "You guys want to talk, or you want to play?"

They played. Two against one. If you scored, you got to keep the ball. The rule was—well, there really weren't any rules. The two guys could come up and trap, or play a little zone defense, one up and one back. But if one of the two of them fouled, it counted as a basket for the guy with the ball.

First guy to whatever won.

It was usually Ty.

Sometimes Will would win if he was having one of his unconscious days from outside, no matter how far Danny and Ty pushed him away from the basket. Will still wasn't all that much bigger than Danny, even if he was a lot stronger. But he had made himself into a better shooter than ever. A *great* spot-up shooter. He couldn't defend very well, move his feet fast enough to cover fast guys. He was built more like a point guard; he just didn't have point-guard skills.

But if Will was open, he was money.

"My outs," Danny said.

"Don't we even get to warm up after our delicious Southwestern Chicken subs?" Will said.

"No."

"Thought so."

Will stayed inside. Ty came outside and guarded Danny tight, maybe thinking about the shot Danny had drained as they were coming up the hill.

Danny started right, crossed over between his legs and went left.

Dusted him.

Will was waiting for him now in the paint.

He hung back, daring Danny to shoot.

No way.

Danny wasn't in any mood to pull up today. He was taking this sucker to the hoop.

Bring. It. On.

He stutter-stepped now, the little move he made when he was setting himself to shoot from the outside, shoot his little step-back fade.

Will bit and moved out on him.

All Danny needed was a step.

All he ever needed was a step.

He was past Will now, going hard to the right side of the basket, planting his left foot, getting ready to attempt the kind of shot he always did when he was in there with the tall trees, one that was half scoop, half hook.

He could feel Will on his side, but behind him just enough.

Too late, bud.

Danny let the ball go, putting just the right spin on it.

Will blocked the ball so hard and so far Danny was afraid it was going to roll all the way down to the ducks.

Will, who could never get one of Danny's shots.

"Woo hooo!" Will Stoddard yelled.

The ball hadn't stopped rolling yet. Danny watched it and thought, *Well, that's not a very good omen.*

He had no idea.

IN THE BOARDING AREA AT JOHN F. KENNEDY AIRPORT THEY'D MET
another kid on his way to Right Way. By the time they finally got
on the plane, about a half hour later than they were supposed to,
all the Middletown guys felt as if they had a new friend.

Tarik Meminger, from the Bronx, seemed to be permanently
smiling, had awesome cornrows, was wearing a Derek Jeter num
ber 2 Yankees jersey. Tarik was about the same size as Will but
looked to outweigh him by a lot.

Please don't say you're a guard, Danny thought.

So he asked Tarik what position he played. Will sometimes said
Danny was more likely to ask that than somebody's full name.

"I may be wearing my man Derek's number 2," he said, "but I
mostly play the three."

Meaning small forward.

"Wait a second," Tarik said to them. "You guys are the travel
team from out there on Long Island, right?"

Will said, "Guilty."

Tarik said, "I was talking to the other two, actually." But before
Will even had a chance to act hurt or say something back, Tarik
quickly put his fist out for a bump and said, "I'm just playin'."

Tarik went over and changed his seat then, so they could all sit
together. On the flight to Portland, it was as if he and Will were in
the championship game of trying to outtalk each other.

The ride from the Portland airport, in an old miniature bus that Will said reminded him more of a stagecoach, took about an hour and a half. The driver, Nick Pinto, said he was one of the counselors at Right Way. When Danny asked where he played ball, Nick said he was a senior guard at Stonehill College in Massachusetts.

"D-2," Nick said.

"I thought that was the strongest of the *Mighty Ducks* movies, frankly," Will said.

"Oh, yeah," Tarik said. "The one where the Iceland coach looked like he belonged in *Terminator.* And then the cute girl went into the goal at the end."

"I still love her," Will said.

Tarik said, "Makes that Lindsay Lohan look like a boy."

Nick waited until they stopped. "Anyway," he said, "D-2 is Division II. I could have gone to a couple of Division-I schools, but I didn't want to spend four years of college sitting next to the team manager."

When he had picked them up at baggage claim, carrying a Right Way sign, Danny had noticed that Nick wasn't all that much bigger than Will and Ty. Now Danny just asked him how tall he was, flat out.

He always wanted to know.

"How tall do you think I am?" Nick said.

"Five-eight."

"Nailed it, dude," he said.

"It's a gift," Danny said.

It seemed like they were only on the highway for about ten minutes before they started taking back roads up to Cedarville, with everybody in the red bus getting airborne again, Nick included, every time they hit a bump. Danny imagined a fight between the bumps and their seat belts that the seat belts were losing.

"You guys are from that travel team, right?" Nick said.

"Them, not me," Tarik said. "The only travel games I play are ones you can get to on the 4 train."

"I think I saw some of the final game on TV," Nick said to Danny. "You were pretty awesome."

Danny said, "Guess so."

"Well, get ready to take it to the next level," Nick said.

Danny found himself wondering if he was going to run into anybody this summer who didn't want him to take things to the next level.

"Because the deal is, just about everybody is awesome at Right Way." Then Nick told them to sit back and enjoy the ride. Will asked if he really thought that was going to be possible without shock absorbers.

"Feel like I still *am* on the 4 train," Tarik said.

They'd occasionally pass through another small town, but mostly it seemed as if they were just taking a long ride deeper and deeper into the woods. Tarik said at one point, "Oh, this is where all the trees are."

Eventually the bus passed underneath a huge arch, like the one at the entrance to McFeeley, with RIGHT WAY BASKETBALL CAMP in white letters on the wooden beam across the top. Now they bumped more than ever up a narrow dirt road, the bus slowing to a crawl as the hill got steeper.

Finally the road leveled off, though, and they were inside Right Way. Danny immediately felt as if they were in some little village that somebody had carved out of a forest. There was a lake in the distance that looked as big and wide as the ocean.

And that wasn't the best part.

The best part was that there seemed to be basketball courts everywhere.

As if basketball had them completely surrounded.

"Okay," he said to the other guys when they'd climbed out of the bus. "This might work."

There was another bus, a full-size yellow bus, unloading kids in another part of the parking lot off to their right. Then another yellow bus came in right behind them. In a car lot way off to their left, Danny could see kids pulling duffel bags out of station wagons and SUVs. These must have been kids who lived close enough for their parents to drive them to Cedarville. He noticed license plates from Massachusetts and Connecticut and Maine, one Vermont, one New York.

Counselor types were everywhere, checking names off their lists, herding kids and parents into a grassy area in the middle of the courts. Beyond the courts, down near the lake, Danny could see a row of bunkhouses that reminded him of log cabins and what had to be the main gymnasium.

Nick said that some kids had come up a day early, on Friday, and that most of the other counselors had all been here for three or four days, getting the place ready. He said most of the college and high school coaches would be arriving the next day. They usually waited until the last minute to show up. It was different for all of them, Nick explained, depending on what kind of arrangement they had with the camp. He said some stayed for two weeks, some would be there the whole time.

"A few of the older college coaches are retired and don't have much to do anymore," Nick said. "So they treat this like a paid vacation in Maine where they can still do their favorite thing."

"What's that?" Danny said.

"Yell at basketball players," he said.

Nick said he might have time to give them a quick tour, but just then they heard someone with a bullhorn welcoming them to Right Way, introducing himself in a squawky voice as Jeff LeBow, the camp director.

"As you can all see," he said, walking through the crowd of people scattered on the grass, "I am *not* Josh Cameron. But he did pass me the ball occasionally when we were in the same backcourt at UConn."

He had a big bald head, and Danny could already see beads of sweat popping up on it in the afternoon sun.

"I had four years of feeling like the most popular player in college basketball," Jeff said. "Because no matter who we were playing, the other team's guards were always fighting over which one could get to guard me."

That got a pretty good laugh.

Tarik said, "Bald dude gets off a got-em."

"Got-em?" Will said.

"Somebody says something funny back home, we just look at each other and say 'got 'em.'"

"Got it," Will said.

"Now, Josh is going to show up before the end of this session," Jeff continued. "And by the time he does, I promise every single one of you will be a better basketball player than you are right now."

Then he said it was time to get everybody settled into the bunkhouse they'd be living in for the next month and that he was going to call out their names alphabetically. After each name he'd call out the name of an arena: Boston Garden, Madison Square Garden, Staples Center, Pauley Pavilion, Gampel Pavilion. Like that. Nick had informed them in the bus that the bunkhouses for the teenagers were named after NBA arenas. The ones with college names were for the younger kids.

Tarik was assigned to Boston Garden. So were Ty and Will, as expected. Danny and Will and Ty were all supposed to be rooming together—Richie Walker had said he'd worked it out with Josh Cameron's people beforehand.

"You want us to wait for you?" Ty said.

"Nah," Danny said, "you don't have to wait for the Ws to get called. Go start unpacking your stuff. I'll be down there in a few minutes."

By now he was used to being in the front of every line, front row of every team picture and one of the last names to be called.

So he waited in the grass while all the other names were called.

Waited until he was the last kid out there.

Waited until he realized his name wasn't going to be called.

When it was just the two of them left, Danny went over and introduced himself to Mr. LeBow, who immediately said, "Of course, you're Danny Walker! Richie's boy, right?"

"Guilty."

"Well, nice to meet you, man," he said. "I've heard a lot about you." Then he told Danny to walk with him to the main building and they'd find out where he was supposed to be living for the next month.

"I think I'm sort of supposed to be at Boston Garden," Danny said.

"Why's that?"

"My dad said he talked to somebody so that me and my friends could all room together."

"Oh."

Now that didn't sound good.

"See, the thing is, nobody talked to *me*," Jeff LeBow said. "We usually like to mix everybody up as a way of enhancing the whole camp experience."

Danny said, "But my friends are together."

"Luck of the draw, pal."

They walked into a tiny office, where Jeff tossed his walkie-talkie on the couch and sat down in front of his laptop. He started furiously punching away at the keys, getting one new screen after another, until he said, "Oh."

Still not sounding good.

"We've already got a Walker over at Boston Garden," he said. "A *Darren* Walker. From Philadelphia. Somehow the computer must have gotten confused, the way computers do sometimes, and bumped you right out of there." He picked up the phone on his desk, punched a couple of numbers, told whoever answered what the deal was.

Then he didn't say anything for what seemed like an hour to Danny. Finally, he said, "Okay, don't do anything. Leave everybody where they are for now, and I'll see what I can do at this end."

They were full up at Boston Garden, he said. Every bed. Like a sellout crowd, he said.

"Mr. LeBow," Danny said, "are you saying that I'm not going to be with my friends the whole time I'm here?"

"No, no, no," he said. "We've just got a thousand first-day things going on right now, is all. So just for the time being, we're going to have to stick you someplace else."

He dialed another number.

Staples Center was full up, too.

And Madison Square Garden.

The whole time they were sitting there, Danny heard voices crackling through on the walkie-talkie. People asking Jeff if he was there. Or saying "please come in, Jeff." One time Danny even heard "Jeff, can you read me?"

Jeff finally just pointed at the walkie-talkie, shook his head and said to Danny, "So it begins."

Then he said, "Do you by any chance have a name for the person your dad talked to? Because to be honest with you, Danny, we usually don't make those sorts of exceptions, even if the kid is the son of an NBA player."

"If my dad says he did something, he did it," Danny said.

Jeff smiled, but it was the kind of smile you got from adults when they didn't want to be having a particular conversation anymore.

Like, *Even if you're right, I win. I'm older*.

"I'm sure he did, and the request just got lost in the shuffle," he said. "Let me work on it, okay? My problem is that a lot of the kids, from all the bunkhouses, are scattered all over the grounds right now. And a lot of the kids in that particular house got in yesterday, which means they're probably unpacked and settled in."

He went back to his computer, punched away at the keyboard again. "Well, here's some good news at least."

I could use some right about now, Danny thought.

Jeff said, "We've got a couple of extra beds at Gampel. We'll put you there for tonight."

"Gampel?"

"Gampel Pavilion," Jeff LeBow said. "Named after the arena on the UConn campus."

"I know what it is," Danny said. "But the college bunks are for the eleven- and twelve-year-olds, right?"

"Right."

"But I'm thirteen."

"Like I said, we're just putting you there for the time being with the younger guys. That's okay for a night or two, right?"

Now it was a night or *two*.

"Sure," Danny said.

That's what he said, anyway, because he wasn't going to act like a baby over this. He'd only been at camp for about an hour.

But what he thought was this: *So it begins*.

It turned out that Nick Pinto was the counselor for Gampel. He was the only person still in there when Jeff LeBow brought Danny over, right before Jeff and his walkie-talkie left.

"I'm like what they call hall monitors in college dorms," Nick said. "Except, as you can see, there's no halls in here."

Inside, it looked like a log cabin that had been turned into a place they were using for a massive sleepover. Gampel was broken up into all these little sections, three bunks to each section, each one with a small dresser next to it. Nick showed him the drawers, like lockers, under each bed. There were still lots of duffel bags on top of most of the beds. Hardly any were unpacked all the way, and there were sneakers spilling out of them, basketball shorts, T-shirts. Some kids had already set up their CD players on the tops of the dressers or were charging their iPods.

Danny liked music fine and had his favorite singers like everybody else. He just wasn't an iPod guy yet. Will said it was practically un-American.

Nick checked out *his* list and took Danny to a far corner of Gampel, where a window faced out to Coffee Lake. Danny asked why it was called Coffee Lake.

"Not a clue," Nick said. "But this does happen to be the best view of it in the joint."

Of the two other beds back here, only one had a duffel bag on it.

When Danny tossed his duffel on his bed, Nick said, "Ask you something?"

"Sure."

"You ever been to camp before?"

"No," Danny said.

"Ever been away anywhere on your own before? I mean, without a team?"

"No," Danny said. "But when I've got Will and Ty, I kind of do feel like I've got my team with me."

Thinking for one quick second that Tess Hewitt used to be on the same team.

"I'm just saying," Nick said, "that even though things got messed up for you, you're gonna be fine. I've been going to sleepover camps since I was eight. This is the best one I've ever seen, by far." He gestured around Gampel and said, "And as cribs go, this is as good as it gets here. Even for the older guys."

"Cribs?" Danny said.

Nick gave him a friendly shove. "Man, you did need to get out of . . . where are you from, again?"

"Middletown."

"You swear you never heard *crib* before?"

Danny shrugged, shook his head.

"Crib is where you put your head down, my brother. Where you do the throwdown with your stuff."

"Got it," Danny said, and then Nick showed him where the showers and bathrooms were at the other end of Gampel, told him the rules about no cell phones—Danny told him no problem, his parents weren't getting him one until next year—and respecting everybody's property.

38

Lights-out was at eleven every night, no exceptions, because everybody was supposed to be in the mess hall by seven for breakfast, which Nick said didn't stink.

"The other two guys in my . . . crib?" Danny said. "Do you know who they're going to be?"

"For now, you lucked out," Nick said. "There's only one. Boy named Zach Fox, from somewhere in Connecticut—I forget the name of the town. He's really small, but I watched him play a bit yesterday, and the little sucker's fast. And good."

Gee, I'm happy for him, Danny thought.

Nick asked if he needed anything else. Danny said, nah, he was good. Then he unzipped his duffel bag, thought about unpacking, then figured, *What's the point? I'm not going to be here that long.* So he just got out his new sneaks, the old school, all white Barkleys his dad had bought for him at Foot Locker a few days ago, changed into his blue-and-gold Warriors shorts—the NBA Warriors, not his travel team Warriors—and went looking for Will and Ty.

He walked past the outdoor courts, painted Celtic green, all of them with lights, Danny noticed. Half-court games, five-on-five, were being played on just about all of them at the moment, and Danny could not believe the size of some of the players. He knew that the oldest kids at Right Way were supposed to be fifteen, so he hoped against hope that some of the guys out there playing right now were counselors.

Because the bigger ones were bigger than Ty, bigger than Tarik. They looked like men.

He saw that there was one full-court game going on up ahead of him, on the court closest to the larger bunkhouses, and stopped to watch it for a second.

That's when he saw Rasheed Hill.

Rasheed Hill from the Baltimore travel team and the travel finals.

He was a lot taller than the last time Danny had seen him, when they'd shaken hands after the championship game. He still had the cornrows, and had gotten a few more tattoos, one even on his neck, just like Iverson. On the court now at Right Way, Rasheed out-jumped everybody for a rebound, put the ball behind his back on the dribble to get himself out of traffic, immediately pulled away from the pack of players around him, both on offense and defense, like he had a gear the rest of them didn't have.

He ended up with a two-on-one, his teammate on his left.

The defender tried to come up on Rasheed at the free throw line, still trying to stay between Rasheed and the other guy on offense.

When he did, like the exact same moment, Rasheed made this ball fake that was so good, sold it so well, that Danny was as sure he was going to pass as the defender was, because the defender suddenly backed up like crazy.

Only he didn't pass.

He just put the ball out there and pulled it back in the same moment and used his last step off the dribble to beat the defender and lay the ball in—no backboard—left-handed.

Danny found himself wishing he could TiVo the whole play, on the spot, and watch it again.

As Rasheed ran back up the court, he saw Danny standing there.

He didn't act surprised to see him or even change expression.

Not knowing what to do, Danny just put his hand up and said, "Hey."

Rasheed took a few steps toward him, then spoke loud enough for only Danny to hear.

"Why don't you come out here and see if you can foul me out with one of your little flops?" he said.

Then he was back on defense, picking off the first pass he saw, taking it the other way.

Danny walked away thinking, *Well, are we having any fun yet?* Welcome to Wrong Way.

Danny found Will and Ty and Tarik shooting around in as cool a gym—outside of a Dean Dome–type gym or the real Madison Square Garden—as he had ever seen in his life.

He should have known as soon as he saw the sign outside, one that simply read THE HOUSE.

It had a high, high ceiling, with all these wood beams up there and huge windows everywhere. They didn't need to have the lights on, even in the late afternoon, because the sun was hitting the place exactly right, like there was a spotlight trained on it. The floor looked brand new, like someone had come in and polished it that morning.

There were no games going on, just a bunch of guys shooting around at all the baskets, the ones at both ends of the court and the ones on the sides, maybe thirty or forty kids in all. The sound in here was something that had always been the kind of music Danny *really* liked the best:

The squeak of sneakers, bounce of the balls, balls hitting rim and backboard, shouts, laughter.

And the most awesome part of The House?

They could pull back the walls on one side, the side facing Coffee Lake, like they were sliding doors. It made a backdrop for all this basketball like something you'd put up for a school play, like somebody had painted a picture of trees and water underneath blue sky that seemed to stretch all the way to Canada, which Danny knew came next after Maine.

Will spotted Danny first and came running over.

"You *believe* this place?" he said. "They should call it The Dream House."

"Where've you been, by the way?" Will continued. "We waited over at our bunk for as long as we could—"

"As long as *he* could," Ty said, "which means about two minutes."

"My room thing got all messed up," Danny said. "They've got me over with the eleven- and twelve-year-olds for now."

"So when are they going to move you over with us?" Ty said.

"Mr. LeBow made it sound like he was going to do it as soon as he could," Danny said.

"How 'bout you switch with me?" Tarik said. "That way you can be with your guys."

"Thanks," Danny said. "But you're not moving. And, besides, us guys includes you now."

"Word," Tarik said, nodding.

He seemed to have his own language, the way Will did. But already you could tell Will liked Tarik's better.

"Word," Will said.

It was getting close to dinner, so some of the other kids were starting to leave. It meant the four of them got a basket to themselves, the one at the far end of the court.

"Hey, I forgot to tell you guys," Danny said. "Guess who I saw playing on one of the outside courts?"

"Who?" Will said.

"Rasheed Hill."

"Rasheed from the Baltimore team? The one you flopped out of the game? No way!"

"Way," Danny said. "And I didn't flop because I don't flop."

"Whatever," Will said. "I can't believe the dude is here. Did he act like he misses me?"

"I didn't get that feeling," Danny said. "Let's just say he hasn't let go on losing the finals yet."

"Tell him to get over it," Will said.

"*You* tell him," Danny said.

Will reached in then, flicked the ball away from Danny, drove in for a reverse layup, did a kind of shimmy that made Danny think he'd come down with the chills or something.

"You know what I bet Rasheed wants from you before we leave here?" Will said. He looked at Danny, then at Ty.

"A rematch," Will said. "With you."

"Hold on," Danny said. "What do you mean a rematch with *me*?"

Will smiled and patted the back of his head, the way refs do when they call an offensive foul.

"Hey," he said, "Ty and I aren't the ones who flopped on the poor kid."

Jeff LeBow came into the mess hall after their spaghetti dinner and announced that they were going to make this an instant movie night as soon as the dinner stuff got cleared and they could push the picnic tables out of the way and bring in a bunch of folding chairs. He said the movie the counselors had picked was *National Treasure* and seemed shocked when the kids cheered as if he'd just made a game-winning shot.

A good sign, Danny thought.

He and Will and Ty practically had *National Treasure* memorized by now.

Jeff said that anybody who didn't want to stay for the movie could scatter, as long as they were back at their bunks by ten o'clock.

Will and Ty were up for the movie, even though the last time they'd watched it together was a couple of nights before they left for camp. Tarik wanted to stay, too. But Danny said it had been a long day no matter how you looked at it, that he was going back to Gampel to chill and would catch them at breakfast.

Gampel was pretty empty when he got there. Even Nick Pinto must have stayed for the movie. Danny heard some rap music coming from the end of the room near the showers, saw a couple of kids sitting next to each other on a bed, one of them working his PlayStation Portable hard, the other kid staring at the PSP as if it were the most fascinating thing he'd ever seen. One guy, he saw, had attached a small hoop over his bed and was shooting a small rubber ball into it, over and over again.

When Danny got to the back corner where his bed was, he saw a boy who had to be Zach Fox, sitting with his back to the room, just staring out at the lake.

"Hey," Danny said.

When Zach turned around, it was as if Danny was looking at a miniature version of himself. Same color hair. The kind of T-shirt with the sleeves cut off Danny liked to wear. Same Barkley sneaks, even. Unlaced, of course.

Danny thought his eyes looked a little red.

"Hey," Zach said back.

"You're Zach, right?"

The boy nodded. "And you're Danny Walker."

They shook hands.

"Didn't want to watch the movie, huh?" Danny said.

"I've seen it like a million times."

"How old are you?" Danny said. "I know Nick told me, but I forget."

"Eleven. In May. But people always think I'm even younger than that."

Danny smiled. "Tell me about it."

No response.

All of a sudden, it had become a challenge, at least getting some kind of smile out of this guy.

Danny said, "Man, I wasn't even thinking about going to sleep-away camp when I was your age."

"Guess what?" Zach said. "Neither was I."

"C'mon," Danny said, trying to make himself sound convincing, "this place looks like it could turn out to be pretty cool."

"It's not going to be cool!" Zach shouted at Danny, way too loud, like a radio was way too loud sometimes when you first turned it on. "I hate it here!"

"Hey, take it down a couple of notches," Danny said.

Zach did, but not nearly enough.

"I don't know anybody and I wanted to stay home and my parents made me come!"

"Seriously, take it easy, okay?" Danny said. Across the room he could see the two PSP kids giving them a funny look. "This is only your first real day, right?"

"You don't understand," Zach said, leaning toward Danny now, his volume switch finally under control. "They make me do stuff all the time because I'm so little. My parents, I mean. Last year they even made me go to acting classes."

Great, Danny thought, *now I'm going to hear his life story because I tried to be nice to him. I should've stayed for the movie.*

"Listen," Danny said, "you don't have to be some kind of rocket scientist to figure out that I know something about being the little guy, right?"

"Whatever."

"And to be honest with you," Danny said, "even though I'm a couple of years older than you, I wasn't all that hot on coming up here myself. But now that I'm here, I figure the only thing to do is give it my best shot."

"But it's going to stink," Zach said. "If I was going to go to sleep-away, I would rather have gone to the one not too far from here that my friends went to, where it's not all about basketball, where you don't get sent because your parents think you're better than you really are. . . ."

Danny saw Zach's lower lip start to shake a little. *More great news*, he thought. *He's going to start blubbering.*

But Zach saved him then, saved both of them, maybe because he wasn't going to lose it completely in front of some kid he just met. Instead of crying, he grabbed the basketball at the end of his bed and practically sprinted out the backdoor.

Danny wasn't sure how to handle this, but something made him follow the kid. Maybe the two of them had something in common other than being short for their age. Because no matter what was happening in Danny's life, no matter how lousy he felt about something—when his parents were having trouble, a bad grade, getting cut from the Vikings—he'd always felt that basketball could cure everything.

At least for a little while.

Zach was on the small, lighted court between Gampel and Staples, already dribbling up a storm, and Danny could see right away how amazing he was with the ball, even as small as his hands looked on what Danny's eyes knew was a regulation-size ball. He went to the far end and shot a layup, collected the ball, came back the other way, pulled up for about a twenty-footer, what looked to be a little outside his range.

Air ball.

It made Danny smile, not because Zach missed, just because of his form, launching the shot off his shoulder as if he were launching a shot put.

The way Danny had always launched it until his dad made him change.

"Yo," Danny called out. "You want some company?"

"Whatever," Zach said when he turned around to see Danny standing there.

"Hey, don't sound so excited."

"You want to play?"

"I do."

"Well, okay, if you feel like it," Zach said. "But you don't have to just because you're feeling sorry for me."

"I never *have* to play basketball," Danny said. "I always *want* to play." Then he made a sudden cut to the basket. As soon as he did, Zach hit him with a pass, right in stride, money. Then Zach broke toward the opposite basket, like he was trying to sneak away in a game, and Danny hit him with a football pass.

Zach caught it and, without even dribbling one time, laid the ball in left-handed.

And smiled for the first time.

Had to, Danny knew from his own experience.

If you were righty, a left-handed layup always made you smile.

Danny asked if he wanted to play some one-on-one. Zach, as if suddenly remembering he was supposed to be in a bad mood, went back to his punk voice, the one with the attitude. "Whatever."

"Oh, you are definitely going down, sucker," Danny said.

How did things possibly work out this way? Danny thought. *Me having to cheer up somebody else after the crappy first day I had at camp?*

He decided to stop worrying about it and just play.

He didn't play his hardest, just hard enough so that Zach wouldn't bust him for not playing his hardest. Danny basically wanted it to be a good, close game, so that Zach's own even crappier first day wouldn't become something for the summer camp record books.

They played until the horn sounded from the main building, the one that meant back to the bunkhouses for lights-out. Zach actually ended the game laughing when Danny made a fadeaway, hold-the-pose shot to beat him 10–9.

Zach laughed so hard that it made Danny laugh, until the two of them realized a couple of guys had been watching them.

One was Rasheed Hill.

The other was a kid Danny didn't recognize, taller than Rasheed. He was wearing a yellow Kobe number 8. His face and short hair even reminded Danny a little bit of Kobe.

"Check it out," the other kid said to Rasheed. "These two musta got lost looking for the jungle gym."

Then he laughed at his own joke and got Rasheed to give him five.

Rasheed said to Danny, "What is this, the JV area?"

Before Danny could say anything back, the two of them walked away.

"Who're those jerks?" Zach said.

"I don't know the one who was doing the talking," Danny said. "The other one is this guy I played against once. Don't worry about it."

"You can probably kick his butt," Zach said, like Danny was his hero all of a sudden.

"I did once," Danny said.

Thinking to himself, *Yeah, but can you still?*

6

Monday afternoon. First full day of real camp at the Right Way Basketball Camp.

They'd worked their butts off all morning in ninety-degree heat, occasionally getting short water breaks—but not nearly enough of them to suit Danny, and he *never* got thirsty or worn out playing ball. The older guys were separated strictly by age today, thirteens with thirteens, fourteens with fourteens, like that, and went from a shooting clinic to a passing clinic to a defensive clinic, even to one for full-court presses, both zone and man-to-man, with a different college coach handling each station. Some of the names Danny knew just from following college hoops; some he didn't, because not all of them were from big schools.

The first clinic was at eight in the morning, and each one lasted an hour. At noon they all dragged themselves to the mess hall for lunch.

Will said to his buds, "If the afternoon is like the morning, I'm busting out of here like it's *Prison Break*."

"C'mon," Danny said, "it's not so bad. It's still basketball."

Ty, who could go all day the way Danny could, said to Danny, "Tell me you're not whipped already, and that was only the morning session."

Danny grinned. "You're right. I want my mommy."

Jeff LeBow came into the mess hall then with his trusty bullhorn and said they were getting two hours at lunch today instead of the usual one, so they could all be assigned to teams. Mr. LeBow said they'd been evaluated off the morning workouts, and now the coaches and counselors were going to basically choose up sides, trying to make them as fair as possible in terms of size, position, talent.

"The elevens and twelves are in one league, the Final Four league," Mr. LeBow said. "Thirteens through fifteens are the NBA, two divisions, Eastern and Western. In that one, we want at least three boys from each age group on each team. Once the games start at the end of this week, if we see we've made one team too strong or too weak, we'll do a little horse trading. But the group you get with today, you can pretty much expect it to be the group you're going to be with for the month."

It was a different place today, Danny had to admit. Everybody in charge moved a lot faster than they had on Saturday and Sunday.

All ball, all the time.

In that way, Right Way was his kind of place.

He felt that way until their long lunch break was over, anyway. Then they all went to the big message board where the teams were posted and found out that he and Will and Tarik were on the same team with Rasheed Hill.

Ty had been assigned to a different team, one that had two Boston kids, Jack Arnold and Chris Lambert, on it, but Ty didn't care. As long as there was a game being played and he was in it, he was cool.

He went off to Court 4. Danny and Will and Tarik headed off in the opposite direction, toward Court 2, the one behind Gampel, closest to the lake.

When they got down there and met their coach, the day only got worse.

Coach Ed Powers, a tall, thin man whose gray hair matched the color of his face, said that if anybody didn't know who he was, he'd been the head basketball coach at Providence College for thirty-five years before the good fathers there—the way he said it didn't make it sound as if he thought the fathers were all that good—had decided it was time for him to retire and turn his job over to a younger man.

Even in the heat, Danny saw, Coach Powers wore long pants and had his blue Right Way shirt buttoned to the top button.

He spoke in a quiet voice, but somehow his words came out loud anyway, at least to Danny.

"Boys," Coach Powers said, "prepare yourselves over the next few weeks to unlearn everything you think you've learned watching what I like to think of as TV basketball. Because if you don't unlearn that junk, you're going to spend most of your time with me running laps."

He stopped now, smiled the kind of smile you got from teachers sometimes right before they piled on the homework and said, "With me so far?"

Will whispered, "No, Coach, you're going way too fast for us."

Danny couldn't help himself and laughed out loud.

"You think something is funny, son?" Coach Powers said.

To Danny.

The players were sitting to the side of the court. Coach Powers came over to Danny and said, "Stand up, son."

He did.

Will's hand shot straight up in the air. "Coach, wait a second. It wasn't his fault."

Coach Powers said to Will, "Was I talking to you?"

"But—"

"It's good that we get this straightened out our first day together." Still talking to Will. "The only time I want an answer from you on this court is when I ask you a question."

It looked as if it took all the willpower Will Stoddard had to keep his mouth shut.

To Danny, Coach Powers said, "What's your name again?"

"Danny Walker, sir."

"Walker?" he said. "Where are you from, Mr. Walker?"

"Middletown, New York."

Coach Powers nodded, started to walk away, then turned back around.

"Oh," he said, "Richie Walker's boy."

It wasn't in the form of a question, so Danny just stood there, waiting.

"Thought I had your dad recruited, back in the day," he said. "Thought he was going to be the one to put me in the Final Four, which I was never fortunate enough to make in my long career. But then Mr. Richie Walker changed his mind at the last minute—or someone changed it for him—and it was the Orangemen of Syracuse he took to the Final Four instead."

Somebody changed it for him? What did that mean? Danny had no clue.

"Your dad ever tell you that story?"

"No, sir."

"No reason why he'd want to, I suppose," Coach Powers said. "But here's what I'd like from you before we continue: a couple of laps around the court. And your friend there can join you."

Danny, feeling humiliated, feeling everybody else on the team watching him, ran twice around with Will, not running his fastest to make sure Will stayed with him.

When they finished, Danny knew the heat he was feeling on the back of his neck wasn't just the sun, it was being called out this way in front of the whole team.

As he stood there catching his breath, Coach Powers said, "When I say run, boys, I don't mean jog like people my age do in the park." He didn't even look at Danny and Will as he said, "Two more."

This time Danny ran like he was in the last leg of one of those Olympic relays, even if it meant getting to the finish line about ten yards ahead of Will.

"More like it," was all Coach Powers said when they finished, before he addressed the whole group again.

"Make no mistake," he said, "we will all be on the same page here, from the beginning of the book. Which is going to seem like the first book on basketball you've ever read in your lives."

He took a whistle out of his pocket, hung it around his neck.

"There's something all you boys need to know," he said. "My team has won the camp championship the last four years. Walked away with a little something they now call the Ed Powers Trophy here. And as unlikely as it seems to me right now, looking at this group in front of me, I plan to make it five in a row a few weeks from now."

He blew the whistle, making Danny jump, and said to them, "Now stand up."

They all did, as if it were a contest to see who could get up the fastest and stand the straightest. "Least we got some size to us," Coach Powers said. "With a few exceptions.

"Players who want to win in basketball get with the program," he continued. "The ones who don't will end up doing so much of the running Mr. Walker and his friend just did they'll think they ended up at soccer camp by mistake."

Danny thought he was already getting paranoid because of this guy, because he was sure the coach was looking right at him as he said, "And from the look of some of the fancy players I saw at this morning's clinics, soccer camp is where some of you belong."

He had been walking up and down in front of them, a basketball he'd picked up on his hip. Danny was almost positive he could hear him creak as he moved. Suddenly he stopped in front of Rasheed.

"Now, from what I saw this morning, I was lucky enough to end up with the most complete player in this whole camp, young Mr. Hill, here," he said.

What, Danny thought, *he's* not *a fancy player?*

Then he watched as Ed Powers handed Rasheed the ball and said, "This is your ball, son, until somebody shows me they can take it away from you."

Danny just stared at the two of them, feeling Will's eyes on him like they were laser dots.

Danny just knew Will wanted him to turn around in the worst way, but he wasn't doing it, mostly because he knew what his friend was thinking:

His ball.

Not Danny's.

Before they'd even scrimmaged.

Coach Powers put his arm around Rasheed now, as if they were already one team, and the rest of the guys standing in the line were another.

"I know they call this camp Right Way," Coach Powers said. "But let's be real clear about something from the start. From now on, you young men are going to play the game my way."

Each bunkhouse had a designated night to use the pay phone in the old-fashioned phone booth outside the main building. Jeff LeBow had informed everybody that they were here to play, not do play-by-play for their parents.

Gampel's phone night was Monday.

Danny thought there'd be more kids wanting to use the phone, but the line that Nick organized—he seemed to put the saddest looking kids at the front of it—wasn't as long as he expected it to be.

Zach Fox still looked sadder than anybody in the whole bunk, but he'd stayed behind.

"I'm not going to lie to them and tell them I'm having a good time when I'm not," he said.

"But you said you liked your coach and some of the guys on your team."

Nick said Zach had gotten the youngest coach in Division I, Bill Brennan from Fordham, who was just thirty years old.

"Just because he's a good guy doesn't mean I want to spend half my stupid summer with him," Zach said. He flopped back on his bed and started rifling through the pages of a *Hoop* magazine.

Ali Walker answered when Danny finally got the phone. And she immediately started asking a lot of Mom questions about the trip up there, his counselors, the food, if he was showering and brushing every day, how pretty the property was, even asking a joke question about where the nearest girls' camp was.

"I have no idea," Danny said.

Ali said, "I could MapQuest it for you."

"Mom," Danny said, "if there is a girls' camp nearby, I guarantee you, Will Stoddard'll find it."

"Excellent point."

The two of them kept making small talk like that, and as they did, it occurred to Danny that he was making everything sound better than it really was, which meant telling the kind of lies Zach Fox was refusing to tell to his parents.

He told her about being in the younger kids' bunk, tried telling her it was no biggie before quickly changing the subject, but his mom was all over him. "Are you *sure* it's no biggie?" she said.

"I practically feel like one of the counselors," Danny said. "It's kind of fun being the old guy for a change."

There was a pause. Mom radar at work, even long-distance.

"You say it's fun," she said. "But you don't sound that way."

"It's fine, Mom, really," he said. "Plus this guy I'm with, Zach, could use a friend."

"Well," Ali said, "he couldn't have a better one than you." Then she said she was going to put his dad on the phone, they probably had big basketball things to talk about.

"Oh, wait, I almost forgot," she said. "Tess called."

Danny stood there in the old phone booth and couldn't help feeling ridiculously excited. But he wasn't going to let his mom in on that, even if she had her good radar going tonight.

So all he said, making his voice as casual as he could, was, "How's she doing?"

"We didn't talk all that long. She just wanted the address up there," his mom said. "I hope it was all right that I gave it to her"—Danny heard the smile in her voice as she added—"even in a time of war."

"C'mon, you know it's not war," Danny said, trying to use the same tone of voice, like this was no biggie, either, the subject of Tess. "It's much more serious than that."

He heard her laugh, a sound that had always made him feel better about everything, and then she said, "Love you."

Knowing he was safe inside the phone booth and that no one outside could hear him, he said, "Love you, too, Mom."

"Here's your dad."

The next thing he heard was Richie Walker saying, "Hey,

champ." As soon as he did, Danny cut him right off. "Dad, promise you won't tell Mom any of what I'm going to tell you."

"Promise," Richie said.

Then Danny told him as much as he could, as fast as he could, about Coach Ed Powers. He was out of breath when he finished, like he'd just had to run more laps.

Richie told him to relax, they could talk freely, his mom had just gone out to the store.

"I can't believe you pulled *him* for a coach," Richie said.

"Dad, the guy hates me."

"He hates anybody who thinks basketball is a sport and not chess with live pieces. And minds of their own. I don't know how this guy got to be some kind of offensive guru, but he did."

"He acted like every single thing I did today other than go to the water fountain was dead wrong."

"That's him," Richie said. "But remember, it's still only the first day. He probably just wanted to scare you all half to death to get you with the program. Even he has to know this is summer camp and not boot camp."

"But Dad," Danny said, "it's not just me. It sounds like he hates you, too."

"Oh, God," Richie said. "Did he give you all that BS about how I changed my mind at the last second about going to Providence, back in the day when he still let his players actually play?"

"He made it sound like you changed your mind at the very last second."

"Don't even get into it with him," his dad said. "But just so you know, I turned them down way early in the process, and then turned them down again after one of their rich alums offered me some money under the old table. I'll tell you the whole crazy story when you get home."

Danny said, "It's like basketball by numbers, Dad. That's not me. That's not ever going to be me."

"You'll just have to win him over," Richie said. "'Cause the guy's probably going to be as obsessed with winning there as he was coaching college. And he'll see that you can help him win."

"No way," Danny said. "Remember that kid Rasheed from Baltimore we played in the travel finals? Coach already announced that it's his ball."

"Take it from him."

There was a knock on the door. Danny saw Nick out there, pointing at his watch.

"Coach Powers is gonna wreck my whole camp. I just know it," Danny said.

Now he really did sound like Zach.

Richie said, "Only if you let him."

"But, Dad—"

"Listen, I'm not gonna try and tell you that you didn't get a bad deal," Richie said. "You did. But you'll figure it out."

"I can't play for him."

"Guess what? You are playing for him."

Nick rapped on the door again. Danny made a sign, like just one more sec.

"If you're good enough," Richie continued, "you can play for anybody."

Danny fired one up from half court.

"Is there any way you could call Mr. LeBow?" Danny said. "Since he didn't get me in the right bunk, maybe he could do something to get me on the right team."

"No."

"No?"

"You're going to have to suck it up, pal," his dad said. "You've had one bad day. Get the most you can out of the drills with the other instructors and then just make sure you show this guy what you've got when the games start."

"You make it sound easy."

"If basketball was easy," Richie said, "everybody'd be a star."

Then he said he loved him and would talk to him next week, and the next thing Danny heard after that was a dial tone.

Danny Walker stood there looking at the receiver in his hand, and for one quick moment, there and gone, he wished there was a way he could make one more call tonight.

To Tess.

Way after lights-out, Danny was sure he could hear Zach crying in the bed next to his. He was trying to be quiet about it, face buried in his pillow. Danny was sure he was the only one hearing it.

But it was definitely crying.

When it had gone on for a while, Danny whispered, "Hey, you okay?"

Silence.

"C'mon, Zach. I know you can hear me."

There was a big moon lighting the lake outside, so Danny watched as Zach turned his head on his pillow to face him now. "Leave me alone," he said.

"Listen," Danny said, "it'll get better."

"It won't!"

He was trying to whisper now, but it reminded Danny more of a hissing sound from some old radiator.

"But you said yourself that having me as your roommate was a good thing," Danny said.

"Not good enough. Besides, I'm only with you at night."

Danny didn't say anything. He was sorry he'd said anything in the first place, because he could see Zach getting worked up all over again. "How many times do I have to tell you I don't want to be here?" Zach said. "Give me one good reason why I shouldn't be able to leave."

"Because you'd be quitting," Danny said to him, knowing it was something his dad would say, remembering the day at McFeeley when he told Will he sounded just like Richie Walker. "And you can't."

"Why not?" Zach said.

The words came out of Danny before he even knew he was going to say them: "Because I don't quit. And you're just like me."

Danny was leaving his passing clinic the next day—at least the coach running that, an assistant coach from Duke, thought he could still pass—when Jeff LeBow came running up and said, "Great news! I found a guy at Boston Garden who's willing to move his stuff over to Staples Center, where his cousin is."

The move, Danny figured, was about fifty yards, but it sounded like some kind of NBA road trip.

Jeff said, "I don't know if I can get you in the exact same area as your friends, but at least you'll be in the same building with them."

"Thanks," Danny said, "but I'm good where I am."

Jeff looked at Danny as if he'd just asked if it would be all right if he could help out cleaning the bathrooms every morning once everybody had gone off to breakfast.

"You want to stay with the young guys?" he said.

Danny tried to make a joke of it. "I'll pretend you held me back a year in school."

"All kidding aside," Jeff said. "You sure you don't want to think this over? Because if I tell the kid at the Garden he has to stay where he is, that's it for everybody. Done deal. Which means I'm done being a real estate agent."

"I'm sure," Danny said.

When he explained it to Will and Ty at lunch, Will said, "Let me see if I understand this. You're staying in a bunk you don't really want to be in and passing up a chance to move to the bunk you *do* want to be in so you can look out for a kid who doesn't even want to be here?"

"Pretty much."

Will turned to Tarik and said, "And he calls me weird."

"He's not weird, dog," Tarik said. "He just sticks."

"Sticks?" Will said.

"That's what you do when you're loyal," Tarik said. "You stick, even if it's to somebody you barely know."

"Word," Will said.

"Beyond word," Tarik said. "Walker here, he's wet."

"I'm never gonna know all your words, am I?" Will said.

"Probably not," Tarik said.

Ty just sat there doing what he did a lot, only opening his mouth for the purpose of smiling at his friends.

The second day with Coach Powers was worse than the first.

Danny never opened his mouth, avoided any kind of eye contact unless Coach Powers was talking directly to him, hustled his butt off even if that just involved chasing a ball that had bounced off the court, and tried his best to learn the offense they were being taught—Coach Powers's famous Providence College passing offense.

It didn't take Danny long to figure out why it was called that, by the way.

Because all Coach Powers seemed to want them to do was pass, at least until somebody finally got a layup off one of the backdoor picks that seemed to be the only thing in the world that made him genuinely happy.

"No outside shots until you get it down," he said. "First team, you guys just keep running it all the way through, and if it doesn't produce an easy two, then swing it back to the top and start all over again.

"You're going to know what to do and where everybody is on the court at all times, as if you've been running this offense since your first Biddy Basketball league."

"And running . . . and running . . . and running," Will said to Danny on the down-low. "They should call our team the Energizer Bunnies."

They were on the second team, along with Tarik, who'd turned out to be slow but was a ferocious rebounder. Rasheed was on the first team, of course. Danny was actually curious to see how Rasheed was going to handle an offense like this, one that did everything except puncture the ball they were using to take the air out of it. Danny was sure an offense like this wasn't nearly big enough to fit Rasheed's game, no matter how much Coach Powers said he loved him now, even if the coach had practically declared that it was as much Rasheed's team as his.

Danny thought about asking him, but Rasheed hadn't said a word to Danny after the first time they'd seen each other. It was as if they were on different teams, even playing on the same team. Different teams or maybe just different worlds.

The first hour of practice was spent going through the offense over and over, Rasheed's five getting a lot more time with the ball than Danny's five.

Coach Powers finally blew his whistle and told them to get some water, because after that they were going to scrimmage all the way to dinnertime.

At one of the water fountains, a safe enough distance away from the coach, Will said to Danny, "Can I say something without you getting that shut-up-or-die look on your face?"

"If you can say it quietly."

Will said, "I just wanted you to know I did notice one guy having fun while we went through ballet class."

"Who?"

Will nodded at Coach Powers.

"Him."

When they were all back on the court, Coach Powers told them to match up with the guys they'd had before. "Now you're all going to do some *real* scrimmaging," he said.

Danny had been guarding Cole Duncan, a redheaded kid with a million freckles from a town in Pennsylvania Danny had never heard of, and the player on the starting five closest to Danny in size, which meant close enough that it didn't look like some ridiculous mismatch. Cole was much more of a pure point guard than Rasheed. Danny had seen that right away, the first day they were all together. Coach Powers had Rasheed at the point, anyway, and didn't seem to mind that even in the big ball-sharing offense, Rasheed still had the ball more than anybody else out there.

He went over and stood next to Cole now.

"Walker?" Coach Powers said.

"Yes, Coach?"

"Why don't you guard Rasheed and have your friend . . . " He hesitated, like he'd lost his place, and finally just pointed in Will's direction.

"Will Stoddard," Danny said.

In two days, it had become clear that Coach Powers either couldn't remember Will's name or didn't want to.

"Have Mr. Stoddard guard Cole."

Danny didn't say anything, just nodded as he and Will shifted positions.

"Thought it might be kind of fun for you and Rasheed to get

yourselves reacquainted in a game," Powers said to Danny. "I didn't see that big travel final the two of you played down in North Carolina, but I heard it was some game until the refs decided it."

The refs decided it?

Danny bit down on his lip so hard he was afraid it might split wide open, not wanting to say something that would get him in even deeper with this coach than he already was, or get him punished into running around the court for the rest of the afternoon while the other guys played five-on-four without him.

That was the smart thing to do.

Just shut up and play. Start trying to win this coach over, like his dad said.

But he couldn't do it. Not when the guy was this wrong.

Not about that game.

"All due respect, sir," Danny said, knowing Will's theory that nothing good had ever come after "all due respect" in the history of the universe, "but you heard wrong."

He looked up at Coach Powers and said, "The refs didn't decide it because *we* did."

Behind him he heard Will say, "That's *exactly* what we did."

Danny turned his head long enough to see Will shrug. His wingman forever.

Now nobody said anything on Court 2 at Right Way. Nobody said anything. Nobody moved.

Finally Coach Powers came over, stood in front of Danny and said, "Is that so?"

As if Will hadn't said anything, as if he wasn't even there.

Danny knew there was no turning back. So he stood his ground.

"My dad says the only way the refs ever decide anything is if you let them," Danny said.

"Well, I'm the ref today," Coach said. "I'll try to stay out of your way, Mr. Walker, let you boys decide things for the next hour or so."

He did exactly that.

While Danny and his team got leveled like they were in one of those end-of-the-world movies.

Richie Walker, Danny knew, overpraised him sometimes. He said he didn't, wanted to believe he was tougher on his son than anybody, held him to a higher standard. Promised Danny that he'd always be straight with him about basketball when the two of them really got down to it, when the conversation was something his dad described as being "point guard to point guard."

"The way all those ex-soldiers say they're talking marine to marine," Richie told him one time.

And most of the time, he *would* be honest with Danny.

Problem was, there was one thing he couldn't overcome: He was a dad. And unless you had one of those psycho sports dads who never thought their kids did anything right—guys who really did act like marines—dads couldn't help themselves in the end.

They saw the player they wanted their kid to be. Or just plain-old thought their kids were better than they really were. They especially thought that way if, like Richie Walker, they couldn't look at their kids without seeing themselves.

So Danny always thought his dad was going a little bit overboard when he'd talk about Danny having "the eye."

Which, Richie said, was something you were either born with, or you weren't.

When the subject came up, Danny would say, "Yeah, I know I have pretty good court vision, or whatever. I know that even when

I turn my back to one side of the court and head in the other direction, I still remember where everybody is behind me."

Then Richie would say, "No, no, no, it's more than that, and you know it.

" 'The eye,' " Richie said, "means you see things happening on the court before they actually happen. It's the reason why the other kids are still holding on to the ball like it's their blankie instead of doing what you do, getting the open man the ball the split second he breaks open on account of the fact that you're already passing the ball the split second before he gets open."

Even when Danny thought his dad was blowing smoke at him, he still loved how excited Richie would get talking deep hoops like this. It would be another one of those role-reversal deals they had between them sometimes, with Richie Walker the one acting like a little kid.

Sometimes Danny would throw one of his dad's favorite expressions back at him. "Pop," he'd say, "you sure you're not overthinking this?"

Richie would give him a brush-off gesture with his hand and say, "Make fun if you want. But with the best thinkers out there, the beauty of the whole thing is that they're not thinking at all. They're just playing a different kind of game. 'Cause they see things and know things the other guys don't."

Except on this day, Richie Walker's son played as if he'd forgotten everything he ever knew.

As if all the doubts he had before he came here weren't just doubts, they were all true.

He couldn't play with the big boys.

He didn't measure up.

He was pressing, he sure knew that, which meant he was going against one of his most important rules about sports, even if the rule sounded like it made no sense: You had to relax to play your hardest, to have any chance at all to play your best.

Danny kept telling himself he'd play through his nerves, the way he always had in the past when he got off to a bad start.

Never happened.

It also didn't help that Rasheed was all over him like a bad rash, all over the court, playing a camp scrimmage as if somehow it were the fifth quarter of their game in North Carolina. And it didn't exactly hurt Rasheed that he had bigger and better ballplayers with him on the first team.

None of it would have mattered, Danny knew, if he were on his game. He wouldn't even be looking for excuses because he never looked for excuses when he was on his game, which was most of the time. He'd gone up against bigger and better teams plenty of times, refusing to quit, like a dog with a bone, until he did figure out a way to win.

Just not today.

Today he was playing like a dog in front of Coach Powers. All his life, Danny had been the one the guy guarding him couldn't get in front of, no matter how big the guy was. Only now he couldn't get in front of Rasheed Hill, who was schooling him all over the place.

The eye?

It was Rasheed who seemed to have eyes in the back of his head on Court 2 and Danny who played as if he had rocks in his head. The more he tried to make perfect passes in front of this coach, show him what a good passer he was, the more he threw the ball away. When he would occasionally get a step on Rasheed and get inside against the two tall fifteen-year-olds they had on the team—David Upshaw from Philadelphia, Ben Coltrane from outside Syracuse—he would get completely swallowed up. Then David or Ben would swat another one of his passes away like they were swatting away the summer bugs that seemed to swarm Right Way at night.

It was why Coach Powers was blowing his whistle about every two minutes, or so it seemed to Danny, constantly stopping the action and pointing out another bad decision or bad pass.

Blowing the whistle and barking, "Time out, Walker."

It wasn't long before Danny thought his name had been legally changed to Time Out Walker.

He wasn't the only one being singled out. Will couldn't do anything to satisfy this coach either. It seemed that whenever Will got an open look, he kept throwing the ball in the lake.

"I thought from the scouting report you were a shooter, Mr. Stoddard," Coach Powers said, surprising them by getting Will's name right.

"Me, too," Will said.

But everybody on the court knew something. No matter how much Coach Powers picked on the other guys, Danny was the one getting picked on the most.

The more whistles he got, the worse he played.

Practice was supposed to end at five o'clock sharp. At a few minutes before five, Coach told them to huddle up, they were going to pretend that the game was tied, one minute left, Rasheed's team with the ball. "Maybe if we do it this way," he said, "the Walker team can get me a stop before we call it a day."

Now it was the Walker team.

Danny ignored him, motioned for his guys to get around him: Will, Bobby Lowell, Alex Westphal, the closest thing they had to a center on the second team. And Tarik.

"Ask you something, Walker?" Tarik said in the huddle. "You slash the coach's tires and he found out about it?"

Will said, "When you threw that behind-the-back pass a few minutes ago? I thought his head was going to explode."

"Forget all that and listen up," Danny said, keeping his voice low. "And just for your information, behind the back was the only angle I had to get you the ball on the wing."

"Still—" Will said.

"Listen up!" Danny snapped at him, getting his friend's attention in the process and everybody else's.

Will's reaction was to break out into a huge smile. "I've been waiting for Coach Walker to show up," he said. "Because I sure have missed him."

Danny said that Rasheed's team would do what they'd been doing all day: run through the offense one time, look like they were starting it again, then go right to a high pick-and-roll.

"Even though we've all been acting like these were the first pick-and-rolls we've ever seen," Danny said, "we're going to take it away from them now."

"We are?" Tarik said. He turned and looked at where Rasheed's team was standing, waiting for them. "Who chose up these sides, anyway?"

Danny nodded at Powers. "He did. Mr. Basketball. But now we're going to give him and those other guys something to think about for tomorrow."

Then he laid out what he expected them all to do. When he finished, Alex Westphal said, "Dude."

Rasheed brought the ball up, Danny on him. Rasheed passed it to Cole Duncan, who gave it right back to him, then ran through to the opposite corner.

Danny was thinking, *He might as well run all the way to Vermont. That's the last touch he's getting, even in a pretend game.*

Rasheed passed it to David Upshaw, now at the foul line, who passed it to Ben Coltrane on the right wing. Rasheed ran through, came back, got the ball back up top. Right on cue, here came David, all 6-3 of him, built like one of those tank-looking Hummers, to set the killer screen he'd been setting on Danny all day.

Except that before he got to Danny, Will Stoddard, coming from the weak side, cut him off.

A defensive guy setting a pick on an offensive guy.

"Hey," Danny heard David Upshaw say, "What the—?"

David's man, Alex Westphal, then ran around both of them, cutting Rasheed off on his left. Danny already had him cut off if he tried to go to his right. Will stayed home, right in front of Rasheed.

Danny watched Rasheed's eyes, knowing what he knew: There had to be a whole bunch of his teammates open somewhere.

As soon as he hesitated, Danny reached in and for the first time all day, flicked the ball away from him, got a real good slap on it, knocking it toward the other basket.

For a second, Danny had a clear path to the ball, and to a layup.

Until Will went for the ball, too, and the two of them collided.

Big scramble now for the loose ball, bodies flying, what felt like all ten players on the court going for it, into it now, like this wasn't a pretend game at all, it was the real thing.

Somehow, pure luck, the ball ended up back in Rasheed's hands on the far left swing, about thirty feet from the basket.

Danny gave a quick look behind him, saw there was nobody on his team defending their basket, started backing up as fast as he could.

Rasheed Hill smiled then, the first time Danny had seen him change expression since he'd gotten here.

Just the two of them.

Rasheed's smile saying, Me and you.

Not exactly the way it had ended up when Rasheed fouled out in Carolina, but close enough. All day long from this side of the court, Rasheed had started off dribbling with his left hand, like he was going left, then crossed over to his right, attacking the basket that way. But Danny had a feeling he'd try to cross him up this time, go left all the way.

And maybe Danny still had the eye after all, because Rasheed *did* come hard to the basket off a left-hand dribble.

Danny beat him to the spot.

Danny beat him there, set himself, ready to take the charge if he had to, or at least make Rasheed pull up for a jumper.

But he wasn't pulling up, he was going straight at Danny and straight at the basket, elevating now, exploding into the air the way he could, putting his right knee into Danny's chest as he did, knocking Danny back as easily as a bowling ball knocks over a pin. Danny flew backward, twisting out of control, feeling himself going down in slow motion, unable to break his fall, and landed hard on his right knee.

Before he hit the ground, before his head snapped back on the court, he had a perfect view of Rasheed continuing to fly toward the basket, laying the ball in, no backboard, all net.

The only thing Coach Powers said after what Danny knew was a textbook offensive foul against Rasheed was, "Ballgame."

"But, Coach!" Danny yelled, rolling up into a sitting position.

"Are you okay there, Mr. Walker?" Coach Powers said.

For the last time that day, Danny felt everybody on the whole team looking at him, knew that if he said anything more, he'd just lose again. He wasn't okay. His right knee was killing him. But he wasn't going to tell Coach Powers that, or act like he wanted any sympathy.

"Perfect," he said.

"Anything else on your mind?"

Danny put his head down, almost like he was talking to himself.

"No, sir."

"Didn't think so," Coach said. "Because I know you want the players to decide the game, not the ref. See you in the morning."

And walked away.

Danny, arms hanging over his knees, feeling as if his head was about to split wide open, didn't move. He was trying to decide whether his head hurt the most or his knee.

Tarik Meminger came over.

"Before I say anything, you really okay?"

"I'm okay."

Tarik reached down to help Danny up, then grinned and said, "Look at you, dog. 'Sheed turned you into a damn speed bump."

8

THEY WERE GIVEN THE OPTION ON WEDNESDAY NIGHT OF EITHER
going into Cedarville and walking around town for a couple of
hours, or going to Casco, the next town over, where the one theater
was showing the new *Batman*. There was a lot more interest in
the movie, so two of the yellow Right Way buses transported those
guys. The other bus and the vans were used for the Cedarville run,
the counselors doing the driving.

The van Nick had used to drive Danny and the guys from the
airport the first day sat eight passengers if everybody squeezed.
Now Nick drove this group into Cedarville: Danny, Will, Ty, Tarik,
Alex Westphal, the two Boston kids from Ty's team, Jack Arnold
and Chris Lambert.

And Zach Fox.

Danny had invited Zach to come along with them, even though
most of the kids from Gampel had chosen the movie.

"Okay," Will said when Danny told him Zach was part of
the plan. "You've officially locked up Camper of the Week.
Congratulations."

"Just be nice," Danny said.

"Won't be necessary," Will said. "You're nice enough for all
of us."

They saw a lot of other Right Way kids walking up and down

the streets of Cedarville's small downtown area, which seemed to extend for about four blocks. There was one general store—it was easy to find, since it said THE GENERAL STORE on the sign out front—that had candy and magazines and a whole wall covered with comic books, more comic books than Danny had ever seen in one place. He'd never been much of a comic book guy—hardly anybody their age was—but he could tell just by looking at some of the Supermans and Batmans and Fantastic Fours that they were real old.

Will bought a Spider-Man.

Ty said, "Hold on. You said you were done with old Spidey after Dr. Octopus looked so lame in the second movie."

"*Spidey 2* was lame," he said. Then he held up the comic book and said, "This, however, is a classic."

He had a way of drawing the word out so it sounded as if it had a lot more syllables than it really did.

Classic was the highest possible praise from Will, whether they were talking about sports or music or movies or which flavor of Ben and Jerry's was best. You might have another flavor you thought was better, but once he proclaimed Phish Food classic, he was pretty much saying the debate was over.

Now he and Tarik, still trying to outtalk each other, the way they had from the day they met, tried to figure out whether *classic* was even better than *wet*.

"It's like my mom says about stuff all the time," Danny said to Ty, nodding at Will and Tarik, "it must've been destiny that brought them together."

The ice cream parlor they found a few doors down from the general store was also classic, right down to its name: Pops.

Standing outside, Ty said, "This whole town reminds me of the

Back to the Future town they went to and nobody could figure out why Marty had a skateboard."

There was a lot of outdoor seating at Pops, and most of the tables were full because the weather was so nice. Indoors, though, was better, mostly because it reminded Danny and Will and Ty so much of their headquarters back in Middletown, the Candy Kitchen. There was a long counter with swivel seats, homemade ice cream being served, even an old-fashioned movie popcorn machine next to the cash register.

Danny was with Will, Zach and Tarik in one booth. Ty and the other guys had the next one. Everybody in the group had camp war stories to tell, even after just three days at Right Way, stories about coaches, counselors, bathrooms, showers, food, the kid in the next bed snoring or making a noise much worse than that in the night, body odor, dorko questions from parents relayed by kids who'd called home already, how this guy or that guy or the other guy was overrated. Or how some fifteen-year-old had blown them away and was just going to absolutely dominate everybody before he went off to Duke or Carolina or Kentucky or UConn.

You heard the word *dominate* a lot at Pops.

Almost as much as you heard about Jeff LeBow's nonstop peppiness and how he seemed to be everywhere at once.

"Lemme explain something to you all," Tarik said. "Nobody is that happy. *Nobody*."

Will said, "Take his bullhorn away, I guarantee you, it's like that deal with Samson's hair. The guy's got nothin'."

Pretty soon they were laughing about everything that had happened so far, filling up the inside of Pops with happy summer noise.

This was more like it, Danny thought, hanging this way, not

just with his Middletown friends. This was more what he imagined camp might be like, even if he had to get away from it for a couple of hours to feel this way.

Tarik was across the table from Danny, facing the door. All of a sudden his eyes got real wide and he said, "Uh-oh. Coach Powers."

Danny dropped the long spoon he'd been using to get the last ice cream out of the bottom of his root beer float. His head whipped around as if it was one of the swivel chairs at the counter.

No one there.

Everybody, both booths, laughed. Danny couldn't help it, he had to laugh with them. And at himself.

"Got you, dog," Tarik said. "Got you bad."

"Only one problem," Will said, head down.

"What?"

"You thought of it first."

"Knew from the first day I met you I had to elevate my comedy," Tarik said.

"Well, you certainly did that tonight with your hair," Will said.

Tarik had let out his cornrows and now had an Afro that seemed to add about five inches to his height.

Tarik said, "Don't be talking about *my* hair with that hat hair you go through life with."

They all finished up their ice cream and drinks, knowing they still had an hour before they were supposed to meet Nick where he'd parked the van. Jack said he'd spotted a video arcade at the miniature golf place at the end of town, down by the lake.

They started walking in that direction, Jack and Chris wanting to know about Coach Powers, Danny and Will and Tarik laying it all out for them.

"Why can't you just ask for a different team?" Zach said.

"Doesn't work that way," Danny said. "They don't have free agency here."

"Man talks about playing basketball his way," Tarik said. "Seems to be because he can only see basketball one way. Like it's supposed to be one of those connect-the-dots pictures we all had to draw when we were little."

"Except when Rasheed wants to bust a play," Will said. "Then Coach My Way tends to look the other way."

"I know you talk to Rasheed," Danny said to Tarik. "How can he stand this guy?"

Tarik smiled. "Doesn't work that way with 'Sheed. He doesn't stand, sit or care. He told me that he can get with any kind of program, 'cause he's seen his man Iverson do the same thing. And he says no coach is ever gonna hold him back, anyhow, any way."

"He told you all that at one time?" Will said.

"Well, *over* time," Tarik said. "The brother said he wasn't going to worry himself about the coach he was playing for, because there's too many college coaches here watchin'."

"There's going to be a lot more of him to see if he's out there for three quarters and some of us are only out for one," Danny said.

Jeff had announced the first day they were with their teams that this wasn't YMCA ball back home. You didn't automatically get to play half the game. You were only guaranteed one quarter in the league games, and whatever you got after that, you had to earn.

Ty said to Danny, "You'll figure it out. You always have before."

Danny said to Ty, "Now *you* sound like my dad."

Ty's response was to point off to their right. "Hey, check it out."

The town of Cedarville was on the north side of Coffee Lake, Nick had informed them on the ride over. The miniature golf place and video arcade were at the very end of the downtown area, in a tiny harbor. A couple hundred yards before you got there, on the lakeside, was a white wooden Congregational church with a steeple that seemed to be the highest point in Cedarville.

Behind the church, Ty had spotted a basketball court, nobody on it.

"You're kidding, right?" Will said, as if he'd already read Ty's mind.

"About what?" Ty said, trying to act innocent.

"Well, look at that," Danny said. "A basketball court. A full basketball court. With nets."

"Oh, don't tell me this," Will said. "Don't tell me that just when we've gotten away from ball, you guys now want to play ball."

Danny ignored him, said to the rest of them, "Okay, who's up for a game?"

Will said, "You've been telling me since you got run over that your knee is killing you."

"I iced it."

"I know you think ice cures everything except strep throat," Will said, "but it's still swollen. You can't possibly want to play when we're on, like, recess."

Danny grinned. "Do you think you're, like, talking to some other Danny Walker?"

They took a vote. Everybody else was up for a game, so Will reluctantly went along.

"One problem, however," Danny said. "No ball."

Alex said, "I think I might have seen a couple at the general store."

But Zach said, "We don't need to buy a ball. I brought mine, remember?"

Zach always seemed to be carrying a ball with him, or dribbling one. Everybody at camp had noticed by now. Even though he kept saying he didn't want to be at basketball camp, it was as if having a basketball with him was some kind of security blanket.

When it was time to leave for town, he had his ball with him, as usual, and didn't want to take time to run back down to Gampel and stash it.

"Zach," Danny said, "you are the man."

"And you," Will said to Danny, "are truly sick. And I don't mean the good sick." He pointed at Danny's knee.

Danny made a move like he was a soccer-style kicker. "Actually, I feel better all of a sudden."

Zach said he'd run back up the street to where the van was parked, be right back with his ball.

"Hurry up," Will said. "We're timing you." When Danny gave him another elbow, Will added, "Hey, I time my little brother on stuff all the time."

But Zach must have taken him seriously, because he was back with the ball in about a minute, face red, completely out of breath, looking totally pleased with himself.

That kind of night, Danny thought. *Even Zach Fox, camp-hater, is happy.*

And for an hour before they had to get back in the van, without any whistles blowing, without Coach Ed Powers busting his chops, he wasn't Time Out Walker anymore. Danny was happy, too. He had Zach with him and Ty and Alex. Shirts against the skins.

Like they were back at McFeeley Park in Middletown.

For an hour, behind the Congregational church down by the

lake in Cedarville, Maine, basketball was fun again, the way it was supposed to be.

The way it used to be.

The feeling lasted until the next afternoon, when Danny's team scrimmaged Ty's team at The House.

Of horrors.

League games traditionally began the second week at Right Way. Until then, the coaches were free to schedule scrimmages among themselves. There was a big sign-up board inside the front door to The House, and getting court time in there was pretty much first-come, first-served. Jeff announced at breakfast the next morning that each scrimmage was limited to one hour.

The college counselors reffed the scrimmages, same as the league games.

Ty's team was called the Cavaliers. They were coached by Tom Rossi. Danny knew Rossi had started out as a college coach, then took over the Hornets for a few years and was back in college now at Florida State. He was a short guy, slicked-back hair. Ty said he was funny, talking from the time practice started until he blew the whistle and announced it was over.

According to Ty, Coach Rossi had told them the first day of practice to pay close attention, he was going to explain his entire offensive philosophy all at once.

"Run," he'd said.

Then came his defensive philosophy: "Press."

"Great," Danny had said, "you get the fun coach."

Tarik had said, "And we get Dr. Evil."

"No," Will said. "Dr. Evil was funny."

The Cavaliers were tall enough that Coach Rossi had Ty playing small forward. Their center, a fifteen-year-old named Oliver Grey, who Tarik said was from the same neighborhood in Coney Island as Stephon Marbury and Sebastian Telfair, was already 6-6, even if he was almost as skinny as Ty.

Their backcourt was the two Boston kids, Jack Arnold and Chris Lambert.

As soon as the scrimmage started, just after four o'clock, Danny saw that they ran as much as the guys said they would, ran as though there were some kind of invisible ten-second shot clock right above the backboard. And even though Jack and Chris were supposed to be the guards, it seemed to Danny that Ty ended up in the middle of more fast breaks than the two of them combined.

Danny saw something else. Oliver Grey had already figured out that if he busted it every time he got a rebound and started another Cavs fast break, Ty would make sure he led the camp in dunks.

At one point, after he had caught a lob pass from Ty and dunked over Ben Coltrane, Tarik leaned over and said to Danny, "I think after this, Ollie's gonna take Ty for ice cream."

After about ten minutes, the Cavs already led 24–6, and Coach Powers signaled for a time-out. Danny expected him to light into the first team for a change. But he didn't.

"That pinball basketball their coach coaches always looks impressive early in camp," Coach Powers said. "But don't get caught up in it. Let them keep running till their tongues are hanging out. You boys just keep running our stuff. Okay?"

Everybody nodded.

Right before they broke the huddle, Rasheed said, "Hey."

It stopped all of them. He never spoke in the huddle unless Coach asked him a direct question. Now he acted as if he'd just been waiting for Coach to stop talking so he could start.

"But we run when we can, right?" he said.

It came out a question, but Danny knew it really wasn't.

"Absolutely," Coach Powers said.

Rasheed said one more thing, to their big guys, Ben and David Upshaw: "You gonna let that Ollie guy school you all day, or what?"

Now he walked out of the huddle.

The Celtics proceeded to cut into the Cavs lead, mostly because Rasheed got hot, and because of the charge he'd put into Ben and David, who finally started competing against Ollie at both ends of the court. It wasn't until there were about four minutes left in the half that Coach Powers called down to Danny and said, "Mr. Walker, give Rasheed a rest."

Talking to him the way you talked to a scrub.

Like he was only here to give the star of the team a chance to catch his breath.

Danny made a couple of good passes once he got in, one of them to Tarik on a backdoor cut. Ollie got over there a step late.

The other one was on the break. Danny fed Will on the left wing for what he thought would be a jumper. But when the defender went for him, Will—already in midair—passed the ball back to Danny, who slap-passed it to Ben for a reverse layup.

The Cavs had most of their second team in there, but Danny didn't care, his team was cutting into that lead, and he was finally hooping as if he still knew what he was doing.

With forty seconds left in the half and the Celtics only down by a basket, Coach Powers asked for another time-out. He called them over, told them to run a play they'd been working on for a couple of days, one he called "Carolina."

Coach Powers had said it was a variation of the four-corners offense his friend Dean Smith used to run with the Tar Heels in the old days, when they wanted to run out the clock. He had told them to use the four-corners to set themselves up for a three-point shot at the end of a half or a game. The point guard would eventually have the ball in the middle of the court, and the shooters would run to their designated spots behind the three-point line.

With the second team, Will and Tarik were the shooters.

The Celtics ran down the clock the way Coach wanted them to, passing the ball around near the half-court line, weaving in and out. With ten seconds left, as if on cue, Tarik and Will ran into opposite corners, Alex and Ben ran to set picks for them, and Tarik and Will came curling around those picks ready to shoot.

Danny dribbled toward Tarik, not even needing the clock now, counting the time off in his head.

Nine seconds.

Eight.

Tarik's man seemed to read the play perfectly, getting right around the pick and cutting him off.

But Tarik, knowing how little time was left the same way Danny did, gave the guy a head fake, like he was determined to get open for a three, then cut for the basket instead.

Wide open.

Four seconds on the clock.

Danny fired about a thirty-foot bounce pass that should have had steam coming off it, even on a hot day.

Best pass he'd thrown at camp.

Wet, as Tarik would say.

But Tarik must have taken his eye off it for a second. Maybe it was Ollie Grey, back in the game now, scrambling to get back in the play from the other corner. Maybe he slowed down to get his feet right.

The ball went off Tarik's hands and out of bounds.

He looked at Danny, shook his head, banged his chest hard as if to say "my bad."

Then they heard the whistle blow.

Not a whistle belonging to either of the guys reffing the game.

Coach Powers had his whistle in his mouth and didn't blow it once. He blew it again and again.

He pointed at Danny, then at Tarik, and said, "You two. Take a seat!"

Tarik, not really thinking things through, pointed to the clock in The House and said, "Coach, there's only a few seconds left in the half."

Coach Powers gave Tarik a look that Danny thought might actually set him on fire.

"Take a seat," Coach said, "or take the rest of the day off."

It was like they were being sent to the penalty box.

Where, as it turned out, they should have stayed.

Because it was late afternoon and practices were ending all over camp, a lot of kids were filling up the stands to watch the end of the Celtics versus Cavaliers.

Coach Powers had Danny sit next to him for the first ten minutes of the second half, having calmed down by now. He pointed out why this offensive set went wrong or that one did, saying this guy set a pick wrong or that guy was slow to switch, see what happens when a play starts to break down like that?

He finally gave Danny a pat on the shoulder and one of those smiles of his, the ones where his lips seemed to disappear completely, and said, "Now, go in there for Rasheed and run the offense I want to run, not the one *you* want to run."

The score was 46–40 for the Cavs when Danny went back out there, along with Tarik and Alex Westphal.

The Cavs immediately went on a 16–2 rip.

Coach Rossi had his guys start pressing all over the court again, and as soon as they did, Danny felt like he was trying to cross some kind of busy street in traffic.

They had done some work at practice, trying to beat a press.

Not *this* press.

Danny kept trying to tell his guys what to do, where to go. Didn't help. Wherever the ball ended up, there was an immediate double-team, or a triple-team, one that somehow always seemed to include the long arms of Ty or Ollie Grey.

The only help they were getting from Coach Powers was this: *"Think!"*

"You know what *I* think?" Will said to Danny, while Ty knocked down a couple more free throws. "I think this dweeb only gets to be our coach for about twenty-two more days."

"And seven hours," Danny said.

Tarik pointed at the real clock, not the game clock. "And thirty-four minutes."

Danny threw the ball away twice. Dribbled off his foot when he tried to beat one of the Cavaliers' traps and get down the sideline.

He'd had one of his outside shots blocked by Ty, which made everybody in the stands cheer.

"Sorry," Ty said quietly after the ball bounced out of bounds.

"Me, too," Danny said.

Danny didn't look at the scoreboard again until it was 75–50 with one minute left. He was wondering by then why somebody hadn't invoked the kind of slaughter rule they had in Little League baseball.

For some reason, Coach Powers called one last time-out. In the huddle he said to them, "Nobody thinks so right now, but this has been a great lesson. Would you boys like to know why?" Without waiting for anybody to answer, he said, "I'll tell you why. Because everybody on this team got a real nice wake-up call today." He was nodding his head. "You all learned a lesson that boys learn the first week of camp every single year—that only the strong survive here."

Will, behind Coach Powers, made a gag-me motion, quickly sticking his finger in his mouth.

"So as we go forward as a team after today, we'll find out who our survivors are going to be," he said.

Then he told them to run what he called the old picket-fence play, from *Hoosiers,* Danny's true all-time favorite movie. He had had the play memorized long before Coach Powers showed it to them, the way he had the movie memorized.

They took the ball out on the left side, near half-court. Danny started dribbling right, toward the stands. As soon as he did, the Celtics started setting their screens for him, one after another. First Will, then Tarik, then Alex, who set a monster one on Ollie Grey.

Danny came tearing around Alex like a streak, hit the baseline at full speed, seeing he had a clear path to the basket now.

He knew how long Ollie's legs were, how quick he was to the basket or the ball when he wanted to be. But Danny had him now, by ten feet easy, maybe more.

He thought about going to his left hand as he came down the right baseline, showing Coach Powers that he could bank in a left-hand layup, but decided against it. He wasn't taking any chances. He was just going to float up a soft little layup and get the heck out of here, go to supper having scored at least one basket today.

He kept his chin up, eyes on the basket like his dad had always taught him, in a lifetime of telling Danny to play the game with his head up, putting what he knew was the perfect spin on the ball as he released it.

Then Danny kept running underneath the basket, the way you ran through first base in baseball, angling his body as he moved into the left corner so he could watch his shot go through the basket.

What he saw instead was Ollie.

Catching his shot.

Not just blocking it, *catching* it with both hands and letting out this roar at the same time.

Catching it like it was a lob pass Danny had been throwing to him.

Ollie was so high, had so much time to kill up there, he actually faked like he might throw the ball down, even if this was the Celtics' basket. Then he smiled and cradled the ball, landing as the horn sounded.

But the horn wasn't the sound Danny would remember.

He would remember the laughter, from what sounded like everybody in The House.

All of them laughing at him.

10

IF HE HAD BEEN BACK IN MIDDLETOWN, HE WOULD HAVE GONE OUTside to the basket at the end of his driveway.

Danny would have stayed out there all night if he had to, come up with a new move so that nobody would ever grab one of his shots like that ever again. He would have taught himself to stop when he got to the basket—"Stop on a dime, get nine cents change," his dad would say sometimes, quoting some old comedian whose name Danny couldn't remember—so that the defender would go flying past him.

Or he would have practiced reverse layups, going underneath the hoop and then going left-handed, spinning the ball off the board, repeating the move a hundred times until he got it right.

He would have figured something out, the way he always had with basketball things.

Figure it out.

Isn't that what his dad had said about camp?

Problem was, there was no basket at Right Way that belonged only to him, even at night. No place where Danny could be alone. It was something you learned pretty quickly at camp: You were hardly ever alone. There were always other guys around.

He'd only been here a week, and already he knew that camp was pretty much the opposite of being alone.

Oh, sure, there were courts and hoops everywhere you looked. But when you did get a hoop to yourself, that never lasted for long. As soon as somebody saw you, it would be like there was some big flashing sign at the top of the backboard: Please come shoot around with me.

He and Will and Ty had joked about being famous when they got here, because of the way everybody wanted to talk to them about their travel team. Now he was famous at Right Way for something else, for being the first kid at camp to get laughed right out of the gym.

Ollie came over to him after it happened and said, "Didn't mean to show you up that way, little dude."

Danny had always prided himself on being a good loser. His dad always told him that if you didn't know how to lose you'd never know how to win. But all he said to Ollie was, "No, nothing like that."

"Being straight with you, little dude."

"Hope you make *SportsCenter*," Danny said, and walked away.

Outside, Will said to forget it, no biggie, it was just one stupid play. Tarik said the same thing. Danny told them he'd see them at the mess hall for dinner, he was just going to chill for a while.

Telling your buds you needed to chill could get you out of almost anything, Danny knew by now.

So he headed off in the direction of Gampel, wanting to be alone. Or maybe just not wanting to be here, not wanting one more person in the whole stupid state of Maine to tell him that it really wasn't so bad, Ollie Grey giving him that kind of diss-down in front of what felt like half the camp.

He passed Gampel, passed the court there, a bunch of eleven- and twelve-year-olds playing a pickup game the way they usually did at this time of day. He didn't see Zach out there but didn't look too closely, either. If he kept moving, nobody would talk to him between now and dinner.

The next bunkhouse after his own was Staples. There was another court behind Staples, one Danny figured would be empty, because the league games, Danny's and everybody else's, had just ended.

But as he came around the corner he heard the bounce of a single ball, then saw that this court was the private property of Lamar Parrish.

Rasheed's friend. The Kobe look-alike in the Kobe jersey who'd made fun of Danny and Zach that time. Danny knew his name now because everybody in camp did, because the consensus among the rest of the campers, no matter what age they were, was that if Rasheed didn't have the most pure talent at Right Way, then Lamar did.

Some other things Danny knew about him, mostly from Tarik: Lamar was supposed to have been on the Baltimore team Middletown had played in the travel finals in North Carolina, but had left the team halfway through the season when his mom had gotten a job at some fancy private school in Alexandria, Virginia, one with a big-time basketball program.

"His mama was just part of the deal," Tarik had said. "The coach there saw Lamar play in some AAU game that fall and wasn't gonna take any chances. So he recruited Lamar *and* his mama."

"Wait a second," Danny had said. "You're saying that this coach recruited a seventh grader?"

"Duh," Tarik said. "These guys see somebody they even *sniff* might be the next LeBron, they show you a first step even quicker than LeBron's."

Danny wanted to know why that same coach hadn't gone for Rasheed, too.

"He did," Tarik said. " 'Sheed's mama wouldn't let him do it."

Lamar Parrish was loud, cocky and, from everything Danny had seen and heard, a bully. Not the kind of bully you'd run into at school sometimes, the kind who went around looking for fights, who acted like fighting was the only thing he was good at. No, Lamar was a basketball bully, one who knew he could get away with acting however he wanted, acting as mean as he wanted or as obnoxious as he wanted toward the other team or his own team, just because he was better than everybody else. Danny had watched his camp team—the Lakers, of course—scrimmage one day, heard how much talking Lamar did even though there was supposed to be a camp rule against trash talk, watched how Lamar's coach Rick Higgins, from Cincinnati—acted as if he was the only one on the court who couldn't hear the abuse Lamar was heaping on any player who wandered into his space.

That wasn't what blew Danny away that day.

What blew him away was how much Lamar shot.

He didn't just look like Kobe, he thought he was Kobe, hoisting up shots every time he got an open look, even if somebody on his team was a lot more open than he was.

According to Tarik, who was like some kind of one-man Google when it came to answering camp questions, Rasheed was the only friend Lamar had here. Now here he was, alone on this court, totally focused on some kind of shooting drill he seemed to have made up for himself, shooting from one corner, rebounding the ball, sprinting to the other corner, shooting from there, a crazy version of Around the World, where he kept crisscrossing the court as he moved himself along an imaginary three-point arc.

It was when he banged one off the back rim and had to run to half-court to retrieve the ball that he saw Danny standing there.

As soon as he did, he burst out laughing, laughed so violently he started coughing.

"I'd ask you to shoot around with me," he said when he finally got himself under control, had even wiped tears out of his eyes. "But what's the point if you can't get the dang ball to the dang basket?"

So he'd seen.

Who hadn't?

"Wait, I got a better idea, midget," Lamar said. "Why don't you make yourself useful, come shag balls for me?"

"I'm busy right now," Danny said, and started walking again, sorry that he'd stopped.

"Busy with what?" Lamar said, his voice getting louder, like he was playing to a crowd, even though there wasn't one. Or maybe he was hoping to attract one. " 'Cause after what I just saw, you can't be busy with no hoopin'."

Danny didn't know why, but he stopped, turned and saw Lamar shaking his head, heard him say, "What I just saw over at The House wasn't basketball. Was more like that beach volleyball. Know what I'm sayin'? Where the little people throw it up there so the big people can slam?"

He started laughing again.

"I've got a question for you," Danny said. "Does anybody except you think you're this funny, Lamar?"

Lamar's smile disappeared. "You smart-mouthin' me, midget?"

Walking toward Danny now.

"Just asking a question."

Inside his head, Danny was asking himself a better question. *Where were counselors when you really needed them?*

Lamar was up on Danny now. "You know who's funny?" he

said. "You are. You think everybody in this whole dang camp isn't wondering how many strings your daddy had to pull to get you in here?"

"If I stink so much," Danny said, "how'd we win travel?"

Danny wanted to step back. The number 8 from his Kobe jersey, the old-school one that Danny knew was supposed to be like the one the old Minneapolis Lakers used to wear, was right in his face. But some dumb part of him wouldn't allow him to take even one step back.

This is how fast it could happen. Danny'd seen it his whole life, a basketball court like this turning into the dumbest place on earth.

" 'Cause I didn't play, midget. That's why you won," Lamar said. "The boy with all the basketball smarts the television guys talked about ought to be able to figure that out for himself." Danny noticed Lamar was palming the ball in his right hand. "So don't be comin' 'round and talkin' no smack about travel with me, or the two of us are gonna have a real problem."

Like we don't already?

"I'm not talking smack," Danny said. "But I have as much a right to be at this camp as you do."

"Well, then, why don't the two of us play a game of one-on-one and see just how much you belong, midget man?"

Then, as if he was throwing some kind of undercut punch, he put the ball hard into Danny's chest, knocking all the air out of him, doubling him over.

Danny couldn't say anything back because he couldn't breathe.

"Didn't quite catch your answer," Lamar said.

Danny, having finally managed to straighten up, said in a whispery voice, "I told you, I'm busy."

"Yeah," Lamar Parrish said. "Busy bein' the camp mascot."

This time he bounced the ball off the top of Danny's head, as hard as he'd punched him with it in the chest. Catching the ball in his huge right hand, he walked away laughing.

Last laugh of the afternoon.

The only quiet place Danny could think of was the lake, so he ran down there, ran all the way to the end of the dock and sat down, feeling like he was still trying to catch his breath. Sat there for a long time until Zach showed up.

This was another time when he felt as if Zach was tracking him by radar.

"Want some company?" Zach said.

"If I wanted company," Danny said, "I would have gone back to the bunk."

It was as if he'd whipped a ball at Zach's head.

"I just thought you might want to hang," Zach said. "Maybe play one-on-one later, like we did that first night—"

Danny cut him off. "Maybe after dinner."

"Okay."

Still not leaving.

Danny looked up at him and said, "Run along now, okay, Zach?"

For a moment, Zach looked as hurt as Tess did that last day at McFeeley, another time this summer when Danny Walker had known he was acting like a total jerk and couldn't stop himself.

Then Zach was the one who sprinted on this dock, sprinted away from Danny. With his trusty basketball, Danny noticed now, under his arm.

From the dock you could walk along the rocky little beach to get to where the coaches lived at Right Way. Or you could take a shortcut through the woods on a dirt road just wide enough for the golf carts that people over there got to use when they wanted to go back and forth.

Danny took the path. On his way over, Tom Rossi passed him in a golf cart, and Danny asked which cabin belonged to Coach Powers. Rossi told him it was number 7.

He was hoping that Ed Powers hadn't gone into town for dinner or gone to the movies or was just somewhere else. His mom had told Danny his whole life how brave he was, as though it were some kind of automatic that you were brave if you were small. But he wasn't sure he could screw up his courage twice to do what he had to do tonight.

He knocked on the door. When it opened, Coach Powers acted surprised to see him.

Or maybe he was surprised to see anybody coming to visit him.

"Well, well, well," he said. "This is rather unexpected, Mr. Walker."

He was wearing the same Right Way shirt he'd worn at the scrimmage, buttoned to the top as usual. The only difference now that he was home was that he'd changed into shorts, which showed off the closest thing to chicken legs Danny had ever seen.

In his hand was a pad of long yellow paper. When he saw Danny looking at it he said, "Used to take notes every night on what I wanted to do at practice the next day. Old habits die hard, 'specially for an old man."

He motioned to a couple of wicker chairs on his front porch, saying, "It's such a nice night. Why don't we sit out here? Would you care for some iced tea? I was about to fix myself a glass before I heard the knock at the door."

"Sure, thanks," Danny said.

The coach went inside and came back with two tall glasses. He handed one to Danny and took a sip of his own. "It's the splash of lemonade that makes it just right." He handed Danny his glass and nearly smiled. "Iced tea, my way."

He angled the chairs so they could face each other, and when they'd both sat down, said, "What can I do you for, son?"

Danny thought, *I came here on my own, and I still feel like I got called to the principal's office.*

But he knew he better get to it right now before he really did wimp out.

He took a deep breath and said, "Is there any way you can put me on another team before the games start?"

Coach Powers drank some more of his iced tea and carefully put the glass down on the deck next to his chair, as if he wanted to make sure it wouldn't make a sound. Then he leaned back and folded his arms across his chest.

"And why would I want to do something like that?"

Danny had his answer ready. He'd been practicing it inside his head since he'd walked out of The House after the scrimmage, practicing it on the dock, practicing it as he walked through the woods to get here.

"We're just not a good fit, you and me, Coach," he said. "It's all my fault, for sure, nothing on you, everybody knows what a great coach you are, what a great system you have. I just can't get it down, is all, probably because I'm not your kind of ballplayer."

Coach Powers raised one of his eyebrows amazingly high.

"Well, there's quite a mouthful. Is that coming from you or your dad?"

"Me," Danny said. "Me, definitely. Absolutely. I haven't even talked to my dad about this."

"Because it sure sounds like something he said to me once, back in the day, not being my kind of ballplayer, like he was some kind of square peg trying to go into a round hole." He shook his head slowly. "Only he was wrong, and so are you. There's no such thing as *my* kind of player. In my thinking, you're a basketball player, or you're not."

"I'm sure you're right about that," Danny said. "I still think we'd both be better off if I was playing for somebody else, and I was hoping you'd agree."

He felt as if he said the last part in about one second flat.

Coach Powers sipped more lemonade. "So you get off to a bad start, and now you want to quit, is that it?"

"I guess you could say I want to quit your team," Danny said. "But I was thinking of it more like a trade or something. You know, one of those trades that they say afterward helped both teams."

Coach Powers leaned forward, hands on his knobby knees, and said, "It's not happening."

"But—"

"Hush now and do something you should do a little more of if you want to improve or learn anything while you're here—which means *listen*."

Danny, both hands on his glass now, realized how hard he was squeezing it and put it down on the deck.

"The team isn't your problem," Coach Powers said. "And I think you're an intelligent enough young man to know that." Now he was talking in that soft voice of his that never meant good news. "Do you want me to be honest with you, or do you want me to be one of those modern coaches who'd rather hold your hand than teach you proper basketball?"

"Be honest," Danny said.

Wondering as soon as he said that just how much honesty he actually wanted from this guy.

"The real problem here," the coach said, "is that since you've been here, Danny, you've gotten a look into the future." He paused. "*Your* future."

It was the first time Coach Powers had used his first name.

"And what you've seen, with your own eyes," he said, "is that this sport is going to break your heart eventually."

Cabin 7 was on a hill overlooking the lake. In the distance, over the coach's shoulder, Danny could see a couple of rowboats. From the beach, he heard somebody laugh. A small plane flew overhead. When the plane disappeared, Danny heard the first crickets of the early evening.

Danny wasn't moving, wasn't saying anything, just waiting to see where the coach was going with this.

Coach Powers said, "I was never one of those coaches telling his players only what they wanted to hear, like coaching was some kind of popularity contest."

All I wanted to do was get off your stupid team, Danny thought. *Now I'm going to have to hear your life story.*

Or mine.

"My dad says that sports always tells you the truth," Danny said. "Whether you always want to hear it or not."

"Oh, is that what your dad says?"

"Yes."

"Well, we're not here to talk about your dad. We're here to talk about you," Ed Powers said. "I don't want you to quit my team any more than I want you to quit this camp. And I'm not telling you that you can't be a fine player in high school. But—"

He stopped now. Came to a dead stop. Coach Powers did it on the court sometimes, as if he'd lost his place or had forgotten what he wanted to say next. The kids would just stand there and wait until he remembered what he wanted to say.

Finally he said, "What I guess I'm trying to say, in a nice way, is that you're probably never going to grow enough to get to where you want to be in basketball."

"What about travel?" Danny said.

"That's the seventh-grade world, son. I'm talking about the real world."

Danny put his head down, almost talking to himself as he said, "I'm a good player."

"I'm not saying you're not," he said. "And if sports were fair, and you were even close to being the size of the other boys, I'm sure you could shine. But sports aren't fair. And the other boys aren't your size. They're not just bigger, they're a lot bigger. And you see what's happening because of that, before we even start playing real games. You saw what happened out there today."

Coach Powers said, "I'm only telling you this for your own good."

Danny wanted to say something back to him. Tell him how wrong he was, that the problem was what he came here to talk about, that he was just on the wrong team. But he didn't. And knew why.

Here was a famous basketball coach, one he didn't even like, putting Danny's worst fears into words.

Saying them out loud.

"Danny," Coach Powers said, "you can learn things here. I can teach you things if you'll let me. I just can't teach you to be as big as you need to be."

The coach stood up then, his way of saying, Danny knew, that the visit and the conversation were coming to an end.

Almost over, but not quite.

Coach Powers said, "Let me leave you with one more thought I had which might sound crazy to you at first, but could be something for you to think on."

"What?"

"Soccer."

The word seemed to float there like one of the first fireflies of the night.

Coach Powers said, "I was only kidding that first day when I told you boys I was going to run you like soccer players. But the more I've been thinking about it, watching the way you can run, well, soccer's full of fast little guys like you."

Danny stood now. He'd thought that Ollie Grey catching his shot that way, then the other guys laughing at him, was going to be the worst thing he heard today.

"You're telling me to . . . to find another sport?" he said.

Coach Powers put a hand on Danny's shoulder.

"I'm telling you to at least think about it," he said.

11

DANNY WALKED BACK ALONG THE BEACH, STOPPING EVERY TEN yards or so to skip another flat rock across the water. Pretending he was trying to skip a long bounce pass to somebody cutting for the basket.

Find another sport, Coach Powers had said.

Not saying it in a mean way, the way he could get so mean on the court sometimes when you messed up. *That would almost have been better,* Danny told himself.

No, this was much worse, definitely.

He meant this.

His idea of finally being nice was telling Danny in a nice way that he couldn't play.

Danny reached down, found a smooth, flat rock, a perfect skipping rock, the kind you could bounce across the smooth surface of the water five or six times. But he threw it too hard, way too hard, so it dove into Coffee Lake and disappeared like a gull diving into the ocean back in Middletown.

Back home.

This sport will break your heart eventually, Coach Powers had said.

Danny was back at the dock by now. It was starting to get dark, and he noticed the lights from what he was pretty sure was the girls' camp across the lake, the summer homes on both sides of it.

What if Coach Powers was right?

What if he was somebody telling him the truth, somebody not afraid to hurt little Danny Walker's feelings?

What if he was an adult who didn't think it was his job to make Danny go through life feeling special?

Okay, here was another what-if:

What if Ollie Grey wasn't even one of the best big guys in camp? What if there were guys a lot better than him? What was going to happen when Danny went up against them? Reach for the sky, his mom had always told him. Well, how had reaching for the sky worked out for him today, in front of what felt like the whole stupid camp?

When Danny had walked out of the gym, he'd briefly imagined himself as somebody who'd just been gotten good on *Punk'd*, imagined somebody running up and telling him it had been some kind of prank they'd pulled on him, that it was all just a big joke.

Only there were no television cameras, because the joke was on him.

He'd never quit anything in his life. He'd thought about it a couple of times. He'd never done it. He hadn't even quit piano that year his mom had made him take it.

But he was sure of something now.

He needed a ticket out of here.

He didn't have the whole plan worked out yet. Just the start of one. And the start of it was acting like he never wanted to leave Right Way, like he was a kid trying to make a team.

That's how hard he tried at every single clinic.

When a ball would bounce away from one of the coaches, Danny would sprint after it. When they'd ask for a volunteer to get back on defense for a three-on-two drill, his arm shot straight up in the air.

When they needed somebody to feed a shooter, he volunteered to do that, too.

At one point Tarik got with him on a water break.

"Yo," Tarik said. "What kind of energy drink you got going for you today, that gnarly Red Bull?"

This was halfway through the defensive clinic.

"It's definitely more than Cocoa Puffs," Will said. "Nobody gets that much of a chocolate buzz."

Danny said to both of them, "You know what the great coaches say, right? You can't coach effort."

Tarik staggered back then, looking to the sky, saying, "Kill me now, Lord. He's done turned into Coach Ed."

In the afternoon, at practice with the Celtics, Danny was the same way he'd been at the clinics. Back home his dad would call him Charlie Hustle sometimes, explaining that that had been Pete Rose's nickname when he was a great hitter, before he gambled himself out of baseball, back when he was the kind of ballplayer all little guys wanted to be. Danny was Charlie Hustle today at Coach Powers's practice, diving for loose balls, playing defense as if his life depended on it, calling out switches louder than anybody on the team, making sure everybody on the second team ran every play exactly the way Coach wanted them to, being the first to give a high-five or a bump-fist when Tarik or Will or Alex would make a shot.

Let Coach Powers figure out if this was the old Danny Walker or the new one.

• • •

It happened about halfway through the scrimmage, with Nick Pinto and a buddy of his from Georgetown reffing, first team against the second team.

Danny had been guarding Cole Duncan to start. Will was on Rasheed, even though that was the world's worst possible matchup for Will; he didn't have the foot speed to keep up with somebody as quick with the ball as Rasheed Hill was. It was why the only time Danny had let Will get near Rasheed in the travel finals was on a double-team.

Now Rasheed was torching Will, both ends of the court, acting almost bored as he did. It was almost as if Coach Powers wanted to make Rasheed look even better than he usually did, and Will to look even worse.

It made Danny determined to get Will some open looks. So when Coach Powers motioned for Danny to call something himself coming out of a time-out, Danny told his guys they were going to run "Louisville," a play that actually gave Danny some freedom with the ball. He was supposed to try to beat his man off the dribble, get to the middle, draw the defense to him, then turn and kick the ball out to Will beyond the three-point line.

It all worked to perfection. Except that Will Stoddard, who loved to shoot, who only played to shoot, whose only real basketball skill was shooting, decided to pass up the open shot and get closer, as if that would somehow make the shot more of a sure thing.

Bad idea.

Rasheed, who had switched over on Danny, switched back now and took the ball away like he was taking Will's lunch.

Took it and started the other way, with only Danny close enough to chase the play.

Ben Coltrane came flying out from under the basket on those long legs of his, filling the left lane, so Rasheed stayed on the right.

Two on one.

Danny was at their free throw line. Rasheed was about twenty-five feet from the basket now. Danny decided to force the action, maybe force a mistake.

Cover Rasheed or cover Ben.

He took a quick step toward Ben, and that made Rasheed slow up just slightly. As soon as Danny saw that, he moved back to his left, set himself to take the charge.

Taking a charge from Rasheed Hill, now there was something new and different.

Only this time it was different.

This time he wasn't just trying to draw a foul.

This time it wasn't one of those things that happened in the heat of the moment—you saw the guy coming, you reacted because that wasn't only the best way to stop him, it was the best way to get the ball back.

This time it was something Danny had been planning all day, just waiting for the right moment. One of the television guys had called him a magician when he and the Warriors finally made it to North Carolina for the semifinals that time. Called him the smallest basketball magician in America. Said it was the same with Danny Walker as it had been with his father, that sometimes he was so quick it was as if he made himself disappear along with the ball.

Yeah, that's me, Danny thought, right before he got it again from Rasheed. Master of illusion.

Trying to make himself really disappear this time.

From this camp.

There was no knee to the chest this time, just because there wasn't enough time for Rasheed to elevate that quickly, or enough room between them. What Rasheed really should have done was pass the ball to Ben as he avoided Danny. Ben was so open he could have headed the ball through the basket.

Danny braced himself and Rasheed hit him ten times harder than he had the other day. Both of them went down this time, Danny landing on the court and Rasheed landing on him.

"Come on, man," Rasheed said, rolling over and off Danny and then getting to his feet. "Is that flop all you got?"

Then Rasheed saw what everybody else on the court saw, Danny rolling around on the ground, holding his right knee.

Holding what he'd decided was his only ticket out of here.

"Stop wiggling around. You'll only make it worse," Rasheed said.

Coach Powers told him the same thing and went to get a towel for Danny to rest his head on. Then Tarik was there, kneeling next to him, saying, "Listen to the man," then getting close to his ear and whispering, "for once."

Danny lay back down. He saw Will standing next to Tarik, just staring at Danny, not saying anything. For once.

To both of them Danny said, "My knee's killing me."

"Maybe it's just one of those stingers," Tarik said. "Yeah, I'll bet that's exactly what it is."

"No," Danny said, wincing as he tried to bend his leg. "I did something bad to it."

Coach Powers was back, with the towel and a cold bottle of water from the ice bucket. "The doctor's on his way. Don't even try to bend that leg till he gets here."

Then he shooed the rest of the players away. "You boys go take a water break now," he said, like he'd forgotten to be tough for a couple of minutes. "It might be the last one I give you for the rest of the day."

Danny closed his eyes, still feeling sick. When he opened them, Rasheed Hill was hunched down next to him.

"Wasn't a dirty play," he said.

Danny said, "Wasn't even a charge. My feet were still moving when you ran into me."

Rasheed said, "Just so's we're straight," as if he wasn't leaving the area until they settled this. "The other day, when I knocked you down? In my mind? We were even after that, for the flop in the finals."

Danny put his hand out. Rasheed grabbed it and pulled him up into a sitting position. "I hear you," Danny said.

"This today was different," Rasheed said. "I thought you were going over to cover Train." It was their nickname for Ben Coltrane.

"We're good," Danny said. "It wasn't your fault, it was mine."

Rasheed walked away.

Longest conversation we've ever had, Danny thought.

Dr. Fred Bradley, who looked young enough to be a counselor, was one of the Celtics' team doctors. He gently probed around Danny's right knee, remarking on how it was swelled up already, asking if this hurt or that hurt. Danny cried out in pain when he touched the swollen place on the outside of the knee.

"Let's get you back to the infirmary so we can take a picture of this," Dr. Bradley said.

He helped Danny up, told him to see how much pressure he could put on the injured leg. Danny said it hurt a lot, but they didn't need a stretcher or anything.

Danny said to Will and Tarik, "I'll check you guys later."

Tarik said, "Word."

Will, standing next to Nick Pinto, didn't say anything.

With Dr. Bradley at his side, Danny limped away from the court. As he did, he heard the rest of the Celtics begin to applaud.

It only made Danny feel sicker.

12

DR. BRADLEY SAID THAT JUST BECAUSE THE X-RAY WAS CLEAR DIDN'T necessarily mean Danny was in the clear.

"I think it's probably just a bad sprain," he said. "But a sprain isn't going to show up on these pretty pictures."

Danny knew that from his dad. He knew a lot about knees from his dad. Richie Walker told war stories all the time about how much basketball had banged him around even before he had the car accident that ended his career. He told Danny that he finally gave up on hoping doctors would find reasons why his knees hurt the way they did—all that mattered in the end was that they hurt.

He sat there thinking about his dad, all the pain he'd gone through in his life, not just in his knees, and felt worse than ever.

"There is a little swelling," Dr. Bradley said, looking at Danny's knee, at the last of the swelling that had been there since Rasheed had speed-bumped him. "But it doesn't look too bad to me."

"I don't know about that," Danny said. "I just know it's killing me."

Dr. Bradley touched the side of the knee again, and Danny winced.

"You're sure?"

"I'm not making it up," Danny said.

I *did* hurt the knee, he thought. Just not today. . . .

"Take it easy, son, I didn't say you were," Dr. Bradley said. "If it hurts the way you say it does, maybe what we should do is run you over to the hospital in Portland for an MRI. Just to be on the safe side."

Danny said, "I'm gonna need to talk to my parents about that."

"About the MRI, you mean? Sure, no problem."

"No," Danny said. He was sitting on the examining table. "About my knee. My dad's got his own ideas about stuff."

"I'm not sure I understand."

"No offense, Dr. Bradley, but I think he might want to have his own doctor look at it," Danny said.

Dr. Bradley shut off the computer screen he'd been using to show Danny the two angles of the X-rays he'd taken.

"How old are you?" he said.

"Thirteen. Almost fourteen."

Dr. Bradley smiled. "Even the thirteen-going-on-fourteens want a second opinion," he said.

"My dad thinks he knows more than doctors, is all. Maybe because he's known so many in his life."

"Are you sure you want to go to all the trouble of flying home, though?" Dr. Bradley said.

"I'm not saying I want to do that," Danny said. "I just think they might want me to."

"Why don't we talk about it after you call your dad?" Dr. Bradley asked. Danny said he was good with that.

"Let me know what he says," Dr. Bradley said. "And you stay off that leg as much as possible for the rest of the day. Keep as much ice on it as you can stand."

He helped Danny off the table and walked him over to the main office. When they got there, Dr. Bradley told Jeff LeBow's sister,

Sue, that it was all right for Danny to make a couple of phone calls, even if it wasn't the designated time for that. This was the guy who'd gotten hurt.

Danny was all set to make collect calls from the pay phone, but Sue said he could use hers, showed him how to get a long-distance line.

He got the answering machine at home, didn't leave a message, tried his mom's cell instead. He heard his mom's voice saying she wasn't going to have her cell with her the rest of the afternoon, she was out on a hike with Horizons kids—underprivileged kids from New York City who came out to live with families in Middletown for a couple of weeks every summer and attend a camp she helped run though St. Patrick's School. She said wouldn't be back until at least five o'clock.

Danny told Sue he'd come back later and that if he couldn't get his mom then, maybe he'd shoot her an e-mail if that was all right. Then he walked back to Gampel, ice pack in his hand, taking it slow, taking the long way down there, along the woods, so he didn't have to pass any of the courts.

So nobody would ask him how he was doing.

The only person in Gampel at four-thirty was Nick Pinto, lying on his bed, music playing from his speakers.

"Hey," Danny said, "shouldn't you be working?"

"Coach Ed's guys are at The House, scrimmaging the Bulls," Nick said. "They already had a couple of refs when we got over there, so I decided to come back here and chill."

He sat up, making room on the bed for Danny, who'd brought his ice pack back with him. Nick was wearing a Stonehill T-shirt with the sleeves cut off, a pair of Knicks shorts that went to his knees, high-top Nikes with no socks, at least no socks that Danny could see.

"How's it feeling?" Nick said, pointing to Danny's knee.

"Not great," Danny said. "Dr. Bradley said it's a bad sprain. He wants to take an MRI, but says he has to wait until the swelling goes down."

"Looks like it already has, actually."

He doesn't seem real concerned about me, Danny thought. "Well, it hasn't gone down enough," he said. "And it's still real sore. And stiff, too."

Danny moved the ice a little, covering the area where the swelling had been in the first place. "I guess it was my rotten luck, hitting it in almost the exact same spot. That ever happen to you?"

"No."

"I just thought—"

"I'm a fast healer," Nick said. "You know how it is with us little guys, worrying somebody might take our spot. I get knocked down, I bounce right back up."

"I'm usually the same way," Danny said. "Until today."

"Until today," Nick said. He gave Danny a look that Danny couldn't really read, like he knew something Danny didn't know. "Anything else you want to tell me about today?"

"About what?"

"Like I said. Anything at all. About camp. About this so-called injury."

"What's that mean, so-called?" Danny said. "Are you saying I'm not really hurt?"

"I'm saying I saw the play."

"So that's it," Danny said. "You think I'm faking."

"I didn't say that," Nick said. "You did."

"You don't know me," Danny said, shaking his head. "You think you do, because you're small, too. But you don't know me. And

116

you don't know what my knee feels like. Rasheed landed right on me."

"And then you rolled like a champ," Nick said. "It's what little guys like us do. The big guys have to know how to sky. We have to know how to fall."

Who was this guy? Ed Powers Junior?

"I'm just wondering how you're gonna play it from here," Nick said. "You know, bail and somehow save face."

"I don't know what you're talking about."

"Seriously," Nick said. "Because nobody's gonna believe what happened today is enough for you to quit the whole rest of camp."

"I'm not looking to quit," Danny said. "I got hurt, is all."

"Right. I forgot."

"Anyway, what's the big deal if I go home for a couple of days and have my own doctor look at it?"

"Because if you do, you're never coming back," Nick said.

He leaned forward suddenly, his face close to Danny's, and said, "You cannot do this. Do you hear me? You cannot quit."

"I'm not quitting. How many times do I have to tell you?"

"Keep telling yourself that," Nick said, as if the conversation bored him all of a sudden. "Let me know what you decide. You want to get out of here that bad, I'll drive your sorry butt to the airport."

He hopped off his bed, starting to walk toward the front door.

Then he stopped and turned around.

"One more thing," Nick said. "You want to tell Zach what his hero's got planned, or should I?"

He left Danny sitting there.

The afternoon session, Danny knew, had to be ending any minute. He figured he had time to go back up the hill, give his mom another shout, maybe she was back on the cell a few minutes earlier than she said she'd be.

He brought some change with him this time, so he could have the privacy of the phone booth if his mom was back on the cell. She wasn't. Same greeting as before, his mom sounding as happy talking about being on a hike as she would have been if his dad had bought her a new car. This time he left a message, said he'd banged up his knee today, nothing serious, don't worry, but maybe she could give a call to the office when she got a chance, somebody would come find him.

Then he went into the office, asked Sue if it would be all right to get on one of the computers and back up the message with an e-mail. Sometimes his mom checked her e-mails when she got home before she even checked her phone messages.

Danny liked to joke with his mom, ask her if she had a secret buddy list for IM-ing that he didn't know about.

She'd smile at him, give him one of her Mom looks and say, "That's for me to know and for you to find out, buddy."

Danny went to the computer room—six Dells in there—and sat down at the first one inside the door.

He hadn't been online since he left Middletown and had seventy-eight new messages. He was about to go through them, see if there was anything worth reading, when he saw that somebody was trying to Instant Message him.

He clicked on the message flag, then the box came on the screen asking him if he wanted to accept an IM from ConTessa44.

Tess.

Danny felt himself smiling for the first time all day. Or maybe all week.

He answered the question about whether or not he wanted to accept her message out loud in the empty room.

"Heck, yeah."

CONTESSA44: Hey stranger.

He wasn't usually the best typist in the world, or very fast.
But he was now.

CROSSOVER2: Is that really you?

He waited, feeling like a dope being this excited, realizing he
was holding his breath.

CONTESSA44: No my evil twin.
CROSSOVER2: Ha ha

He started to type something else. As he did, the message came
up in red that his buddy was typing something, too. So it was like
the old days now, him and Tess Hewitt trying to beat each other to
the next funny comment.
Only she wasn't trying to be funny.
Just Tess.

CONTESSA44: So how are you stranger? How's camp?
CROSSOVER2: Great.

He waited, getting the "Your buddy is typing" message.

CONTESSA44: Great as in offthecharts travel team great?
That great?
CROSSOVER2: Well getting there I guess.

This wait seemed to be longer.

ConTessa44: You guess? You never guess in bball fella. You always have the right answer. Before they even ask the question sometimes.
Crossover2: I used to.
ConTessa44: USED TO????? Past tense.
Crossover2: Maybe just tense.
ConTessa44: Hey you. Something wrong?

Truth or dare? Tell her the truth now, or not.
Danny decided on the truth.
He needed to tell somebody the truth today.

Crossover2: Hate it here. Got hurt today.

He didn't tell her he was leaving.
This time Danny waited for what seemed like an hour while his buddy was typing.

ConTessa44: Come on Walker. Only a week. How bad can it be? It'll get better. Then you'll win. Like always.
Crossover2: Not this time. No no no.
ConTessa44: Yes yes YES!

He wasn't in the mood for a pep talk, not even from her.
So he changed the subject.

Crossover2: How's Middletown?
ConTessa44: Have no idea.

He closed his eyes, searching what was left of his brain. Was there a trip she was taking somewhere? Danny tried to remember if she'd said anything about that the last time they talked.

Then he decided he really didn't care where she was.

All he cared about was that they were talking again, even like this.

CROSSOVER2: Okay I give. Where R U?

He didn't have to wait long.

CONTESSA44: Across the lake.

13

WILL AND TY WERE PLAYING PING-PONG AT THE OUTDOOR TABLE BE-hind Boston Garden when Danny found them.

Will gave Danny a sideways look and said, "Oh, you're still here?"

Danny said, "I'm here."

"Because we were wondering."

"You guys don't have to wonder about me."

"If you say so."

"I say so."

"Hello?" Ty said. "Are we still playing to twenty-one, or are we stopping now?"

Will was getting ready to serve when Danny said, "I've got some news I thought you might be interested in."

Will held the pose as if Danny had paused him. "About your knee?"

"No," Danny said, "nothing about my knee. I'm tired of talking about my knee today."

"The reason I ask," Will said, going right on, "is that we ran into Nick Pinto and he said you might be fixing to leave and I just thought that might be something you'd want to mention to your two best friends before you did. Is all."

"Because if you want to quit—" Ty said.

"I'm not quitting!" Danny said.

"Chill," Ty said, holding up his racket like a stop sign. "I was talking to Will about our game."

Will started his service motion again. Paused again. Danny heard Ty groan. "What's your news, then?"

"Tess is across the lake."

That got his attention.

"No way."

"Way," Danny said. He grinned and pointed toward the lake. "Thataway, actually."

"How?" Will said.

"Her uncle," Danny said. "When we were sitting at McFeeley one day, she laughed when I told her our camp was in Cedarville. It turned out she couldn't believe we were going to be right near where her uncle has a place."

Will said to Ty, "No wonder he seems to have recovered from his near-death experience."

"Tess to the rescue," Ty said.

"So when do we get to see her?" Will said.

"Tonight."

"How?"

Danny said to his buds, "We'll know that as soon as we come up with a plan."

Most of the guys bunking at Boston Garden were over at The House by now, watching the nightly counselors' game.

Danny and Will and Ty were sitting on some big rocks at the edge of the woods, overlooking the water.

Danny told them that according to Tess, her uncle's place was a couple of miles away if you went the long way, which meant by car. But she said it was actually a lot closer if you went across Coffee Lake, maybe halfway between Right Way and the girls' camp across the water.

"Too far to swim," Will said.

"Ya think?" Ty said.

"So we'll take a canoe," Will said, "definitely." Nodding his head quickly—Will was completely happy talking to himself—"Brilliant," he said.

"Oh, right," Danny said. "They're just going to let us take a canoe out at this time of night."

Will looked at him like he was the biggest loser on earth.

"We're not going out on the lake now," he said. "We're going to wait until it gets dark, and then we're going to steal one of these long, skinny boats, and *then* we're going to see our friend Tess Hewitt."

"We're stealing a boat," Danny said.

"Well, borrowing," Will said. "I don't intend to keep it. What am I going to do with a canoe?"

"We get it," Danny said.

Ty said, "Why don't we just wait until the counselors' game is over and then ask Nick or somebody to drive us?"

"First of all, nobody ever knows when the counselors' game is going to end," Will said. "Sometimes they play until ten o'clock."

Will Stoddard smiled then, looking at Danny, then Ty, then back at Danny, his eyes, as always, full of fun and trouble at the same time.

"Second, and most importantly," Will said, "if Nick or somebody just plain old drove us over to her in the van, what kind of adventure would that be?"

Danny and Ty told him they hated to admit it, but he made a good point.

Danny said there was still time before it got all the way dark, so he went back to call Tess, tell her the plan they'd come up with, figure out exactly which place was her uncle's and how they were going to find it in the dark.

When he got to the main office, Sue LeBow said, "Where have you been? I had people looking all over the camp for you. Your mom called and wants you to call her right away."

Danny said he'd been hanging with his friends. Sue said he was lucky he showed up when he did; she was about to close up the office for the night. He could go ahead and use her phone while she went over to the mess hall to get a cup of coffee.

Danny didn't have a whole lot of time to waste, he knew, but he also knew he better make the call.

She picked up on the first ring.

"Hey, Mom."

"How bad is it?"

Not his cool, funny mom tonight. This was the mom who got right to it on the big stuff, like she was calling one of her English classes to order.

If she had been home when Danny called before, he had planned to start scamming a trip home to see the family doctor. But now he didn't want to even think about that, he just wanted to go see Tess. So he told Ali Walker about the play, about Dr. Bradley, about how he'd taken it easy the rest of the day, tried to make it sound as if he'd been icing for the last four hours straight.

"I'll live, basically," he said. "The doctor says he might want to go for an MRI when the swelling goes down."

"Good Lord," Ali Walker said, "what is it about the men in this family and their knees?"

"Mom," he said, "one bruised knee doesn't mean I've turned into Dad."

There was a pause, and then his mom said, "Do you want me to call your dad? He's still in Oakland until tomorrow night."

Quickly, maybe too quickly with his mom on the other end of the line, the way she could hear things in his voice that no other living human could hear, Danny said, "Why don't you wait until he gets home? Let me see how it feels tomorrow, and I'll call you guys."

His mom said, "No basketball until it feels better. Do you hear me, Daniel Walker?"

"Loud and clear."

"You promise your old mom?"

"Yes," he said—never "yeah," not with an English teacher for a mother. "And you're not old."

"And you're sweet, even with a bum knee."

"Hey, Mom?" Danny said. "I love you a lot, but the guys are waiting for me to go do something."

"Well," she said. "The guys. Waiting to do *something*. I wouldn't want to stand in the way of all *that*."

"Did I mention that you're not old?" Danny said.

"I love you, good-bye," she said.

After he'd hung up, he realized he hadn't even told her about Tess. Maybe tomorrow. He called Tess then, got the exact directions, even drew himself a crude map from what she was telling him about her part of Coffee Lake.

On his way back to where Will and Ty were waiting, he saw Zach playing a three-on-three game on the lighted court at Gampel. Danny knew he shouldn't stop, but he did, still feeling bad about the way he'd treated Zach on the dock.

When one of the other kids made a driving shot to win the game, Danny motioned Zach over.

"What'd I do now?" Zach said.

"Nothing," Danny said. "I just wanted to talk to you about something."

"What?"

The night before, when Danny had gotten back to Gampel, Zach had pretended to be asleep, even though Danny knew better.

"I want to talk about an adventure," Danny said, then pulled him out of earshot of the other guys and told him what they planned on doing.

"You're asking me to come along?" Zach said.

"Unless you don't want to."

"Are you insane?" Zach said. "Just give me one sec to put my ball away." By now Danny knew that you could have gone into Zach's living space at Gampel and taken all his clothes and games and whatever money he had hidden and the only thing he'd be upset about would be his basketball.

On their way down to the water, Zach said, "Nick was talking about your knee before—"

Danny thought, *Who hasn't Nick spilled the beans to?* But he just said, "I'll tell you all about it tomorrow. Right now, it's time to hit the high seas."

Zach Fox looked at him. "Now *that,*" he said, "really is wet."

The counselor in charge of sending you out in the canoes was long gone by the time it was all the way dark. Nobody had a watch, but they guessed it was past nine o'clock when they snuck back down to the dock.

There were six canoes tied up there, paddles inside. On the other side of the dock were two Jet Skis.

"We could get there a lot faster on these very cool-looking Jet Skis," Will said. "Plus, it would be like a chase scene in James Bond."

"Faster and much, much louder," Danny said.

"I'm not looking to change the plan," Will said. "I was just making what I thought was an interesting observation."

"There's something new and different," Ty said.

Zach wasn't saying anything. He was just smiling at all of them at once in the light of a pretty amazing full moon, looking as happy as Danny had seen him without a basketball in his hands.

They sent Zach up the hill one last time, to make sure nobody was coming. He came racing back like he was trying to set the camp record and said the coast was clear.

"Well, then," Danny said, "I guess it's time to ship out."

They untied the canoe closest to the dock as Will asked for about the tenth time if Danny was sure where they were going.

"Sort of."

"Well, let's sort of start heading over there," Will said, "so we at least have a chance to get back before somebody realizes none of us are in our beds."

"Have any of you guys ever ridden in one of these?" Zach said.

Danny shook his head and looked at Will and Ty.

"Don't look at me," Will said. "My mom swears she used to take me kayaking when I was little, but I told her I was gonna have to see pictures."

From his seat at the front of the boat, Ty said, "I can do it."

"Should have known," Will said to Zach. "He could fly a plane if he had to."

Ty explained then that these were what were known as "guide canoes," because they were a favorite of Maine tour guides, and were about sixteen feet long. Will wanted to know how Ty knew that, and Ty said, "When you're not one of those people who *already* know everything, you ask questions sometimes."

"Is that a shot?" Will said. "Because that sounded like a shot to me."

There were four life jackets in the bottom of the boat, two of which were small enough to fit Danny and Zach. Ty said that the most people he'd seen in one of these babies since he'd been at camp were three, but there was nothing to worry about, guide canoes like this could handle up to six hundred pounds.

Will made a motion like he was writing a score on a board and said to Ty, "Okay, I get it. You've got me beat bad on canoes."

"And just about everything else," Danny added.

"Another shot," Will said.

Ty stayed in front, Danny said he'd handle the paddling in back, maybe switch with Will if he got tired.

"I'm going to be pretty busy navigating," Will said.

They pushed away into Coffee Lake, the only real sound in the night the sound of their paddles hitting the water. Danny had already told Will to keep his voice down as much as possible, that out here on the water it would carry better than if he were using Jeff's bullhorn.

They angled to their left, past the rope line you weren't supposed to cross if you had permission to take one of the canoes out, went around a bend and the Right Way dock disappeared from sight. They were five minutes into the trip, if that.

Will said, "Are we there yet?"

Danny and Ty were already in perfect sync with their paddling, as if they were on some kind of two-man rowing team in the Olympics. Or maybe just running one of their little two-man games on a basketball court.

"Hey, you guys are good," Zach said. "Danny, you sure you've never done this before?"

"Suck-up," Will said into his hand, like he was stifling a cough.

They glided across the water in the night, moving faster than Danny thought they would, still just hearing the slap of the paddles when Will piped down. Danny switched the paddle from side to side, feeling strong as he did.

Realizing something at the same time:

It was like they were out here in their own little world, apart from camp. He wasn't worried about anything, he wasn't mad at anybody, he wasn't all jammed up about what he'd decided to do before Tess called.

He would never say this out loud, certainly not to Will or Ty, not to Zach in a million years, but out here on Coffee Lake, Danny suddenly felt like he was floating.

Just then, Ty said, "There she is."

Tess had told Danny she'd come out to the end of her uncle's dock and be carrying one of those supersize flashlights that you only used when you lost power.

He was maybe a hundred yards away from her.

Will asked if it was all right for him to give her a shout-out now. The only way somebody from Right Way would be able to hear was if they'd been followed.

"Knock yourself out," Danny told him.

Will waved now and yelled, "Hilary Duff, is that you? Is it really you?"

"Hey!" Tess yelled back. Danny could see her flashlight bouncing up and down now as she did. "Hey, you guys!"

Will said to Danny, "Jump in anytime."

Without either one of them saying anything about picking up the pace, Danny and Ty both started paddling faster.

"Just pull alongside the dock," Tess said, "and I'll toss you a rope."

Maybe thirty yards away now.

Now Danny couldn't help himself.

Or contain himself.

After all the bad parts, he'd come to the good parts, finally.

Tess.

He tapped Will on his shoulder, handed him his paddle, stood up in the back of the boat. Usually he was soooooo cool toward Tess when Will and Ty were around, never acting like he was too happy or excited to see her.

Not tonight.

He shouted "ConTessa44 Hewitt!" at the top of his voice, waving his arm like he was calling for somebody to pass him the ball.

Will was standing now, giving Danny room to take his seat. But Danny didn't want to sit in it, he wanted to stand on it, wanted to be the tallest one in the boat for just this one moment.

Wanted Tess to see him first.

There was just one small problem.

Just enough water from the splash of those paddles had gotten into the bottom of the boat on their way across the lake.

It meant that Danny's Barkley sneakers were just slick enough.

His right sneaker got up on the little benchlike seat, no problem. But his left one slipped like he'd hit a patch of ice. And since there was no rail for him to grab on to, nothing but the night air for him to grab on to, Danny felt himself falling.

Zach saw what was happening, tried to dive across and catch him, but it was too late.

Danny Walker went over the side of the guide canoe and into the cold water of Coffee Lake.

THE FIRST VOICE DANNY HEARD AS HIS HEAD POPPED BACK ABOVE the surface was Will Stoddard's. "No worries, Tess. Your hero has arrived."

Ty reached over and helped Danny back into the boat, saying, "You know, when Will said to jump in anytime, I don't think this is what he had in mind."

Everybody in the canoe laughed then. As foolish as Danny felt in front of Tess, like he was the entertainment at SeaWorld, he had to join in. They all kept laughing until they got the canoe to the side of Tess's dock and she tossed Ty the rope.

"You sure know how to make an entrance, Walker," Tess said as she reached out to give him a hand.

"I think I might've held my tuck a little too long," he said.

Tess waved her arms above her head like a crazy person, doing this spazzy puppet dance. "Is that what they call a tuck now in diving?" she said.

She was wearing the gray Warriors sweatshirt they'd given her as an honorary member of the team after they'd won the travel championship, jeans with holes in both knees and what looked to be new Puma sneakers. Danny could spot new sneakers even in the dark.

And he knew it didn't matter what she was wearing, here or anywhere, she always looked great to him.

He thought, she's the same old Tess.

And I'm a mess.

On the dock, Will told Danny he should look on the bright side, despite the way he'd been playing lately, especially for his new coach.

"See, you *can* hit the water if you fall out of a boat," Will said.

"Not funny," Danny said.

"Well, we both know *that's* a total lie," Will said.

Everybody was talking at once then, Danny introducing Zach to Tess, Will saying they called him Danny Junior, Tess saying she could see why, Tess wanting to know if she should try to find Danny some dry clothes and Danny saying, no, he was fine, which was a total lie.

Tess said her aunt and her two cousins had gone into town for ice cream, but that her uncle was inside watching the Red Sox–Yankees game if anybody wanted to join him. She was sure he'd love the company.

"Television," Will said, making it sound as if he were talking about heaven.

"Not just television," Tess said. "He's got Direct up here."

"Yessssss!" Will said, pumping his fist. "What kind of snacks we talking about?"

Tess said that her two cousins were boys, one twelve and one fourteen, so there was more junk food in the kitchen than you could imagine. Her aunt had taken them grocery shopping the day before and let them go wild.

Will said, "I am so there with my new best friend, Uncle . . . ?"

"Sam."

Then because he was Will, because he still had Danny's back, he immediately shoved Ty and Zach in the direction of The House and said, "Let's leave these two guys alone for a few minutes. Walker probably wants to show Tess his backflip next."

Over his shoulder, Will said, "Call us if you need us."

"We won't," Danny said. "Call you or need you."

When they were gone, Tess sprinted down the dock on her long legs, disappeared through the backdoor, came right back out with two huge red beach towels.

"You must be freezing to death," she said.

"You see now why Will says I turn into Captain Klutz when you're around."

"Nah," Tess said. "I'm still just seeing the captain of the team."

"Not lately," Danny said.

"You want to talk about it?" she said.

Danny said she had no idea.

They sat on the back porch in old rickety, squeaky, wooden rocking chairs, Danny feeling like some kind of old man with the red towel over his shoulders. From the television room at the front of The House, the only voice he'd hear occasionally was Will's, no shocker. From somewhere in the woods, they could hear an owl making hoot noises, as if saying that all these people had crashed his night.

Danny said that before he told Tess about everything that was going on at camp, he needed to apologize for something. Tess started to say he didn't, but Danny kept right on going, saying he had been the kind of jerk that even real jerks thought was obnoxious the last time he'd seen her.

She smiled.

"Oh, come on now," she said. "You're being much too easy on yourself."

"Very funny," he said, smiling back. "I get Will the comedian all day and now you at night."

"You lucky dog."

"Only if you mean a wet, mangy-type dog."

They sat there rocking and squeaking.

"I mean it," Danny said. "About being sorry."

"I know."

"Scott bugs me, is all. But you probably know that, too."

"I do."

"I can't help it."

Tess said, "He's actually not a bad guy, if you don't mind complete perfection."

Danny wanted to say it had never bothered him with her but kept that particular thought inside his head. The way he kept a lot of thoughts like that, about this girl, inside his head.

"You also have to care a lot more about Roger Federer than I do," Tess said.

"So you don't want to be the queen of Middletown tennis anymore?"

"I guess I'll wait until next summer to win Wimbledon," Tess said, then quickly told him how bored she got after he and Will and Ty left, and how after about two days of her moping around the house, her mom said she needed some kind of outing. Which, Tess knew, meant some kind of road trip. That night she got on her computer, MapQuested how far away her uncle actually was from Right Way, discovered the distance was 1.8 miles and now here she was, surprise!

For once, he wasn't Captain Klutz.

"I'm glad you're here," he said.

"I also know that," Tess said. "Now tell me some stuff I don't know."

Danny talked for a long time. Told her all about it, all the gory details. Finally admitted to her that Nick Pinto had been right when he'd called him out, that Danny had tricked up his knee injury, knowing his knee was already swollen even if it wasn't bothering him anymore, figuring it was the easiest way for him to get the heck out of there without looking like a total wussball.

Tess never said a word the whole time he was talking, never interrupted him once. Never looked anywhere except right at him and right through him.

When he finished, she said, "So do you want to know what I really think?"

"It's why we hijacked that dopey boat," Danny said. "Course I want to know what you think."

"Well, I think . . ." She scratched her head, paused briefly, like she was confused. "I think . . . that if you ever think about doing something this stupid ever again, I will personally break *both* your knees."

She went inside, came back with two bottles of Snapple and handed him one. She'd also brought him two more dry towels, even though he'd said he was okay with what he had.

"It can't be as bad as you say," Tess said.

"Really?" he said. "Well, guess what. The only time I really felt like I wanted to be at this stupid camp was tonight. And tonight what we basically did was get away from camp. And come to see you."

"You just have to show this guy," she said. "This Coach Ed."

"What if he's right about me?"

"He's not."

Just like that. Like she was saying, Case closed, done deal, next question.

"You don't know that," Danny said.

"I know you, Walker. I know you better than anybody. I know you better than he ever will. Or any coach ever will, outside of your dad, when you start playing for him. But you're acting like this Coach Ed is suddenly the world's expert on Danny Walker, that he has all these big insights into you that the rest of us don't. Get real."

Danny said, "How about I just get out?" Knowing how weak that sounded.

Air ball.

"You can't quit," Tess said.

"So I bang my head against the wall for two more weeks, with a coach who acts like he only wants to put me into games as some kind of last resort," Danny said.

He heard a war whoop from Will inside, which meant the Red Sox had done something. Will and Zach were Red Sox fans, Ty was a huge Yankees fan. Danny didn't know where Uncle Sam weighed in.

Tess said, "You know what this really is? It's Ty's dad cutting you all over again. Another grown-up telling you you're not good enough. I thought you always used to tell me that the championship you guys really won in travel was the championship of any kid who got told by an adult they weren't good enough?"

Danny knew he was smiling. He couldn't help himself, even after the two crummiest days on record. She never forgot anything. She remembered Danny's life better than he did sometimes.

"It's my dad's line, actually."

"So now you have to do that again," Tess said. "You show him, you show the whole camp, if you have to. You show this guy Rasheed who keeps knocking you down. You're not quitting, and you're not believing something from this coach you know isn't true and I know isn't true."

Danny wanted a ball in his hands now. Wished he'd let Zach bring his ball with him, so he could hold it, roll it around in his hands, dribble it on the back porch, flick it straight up in the air. A ball in his hands had always made him feel smarter, even smart enough to keep up with Tess. A ball in Danny's hands had always made him feel that he could figure anything out, like it was just a simple basketball problem, finding the smartest way to get the ball from here to there and then through the hoop.

"You didn't hear them laughing at me in the gym," he said quietly.

"For one play," Tess said. "One stupid play. Ty broke his wrist once because of one stupid play that wasn't even your fault." Tess shrugged, smiled. "Get over it, Walker."

There was a rap on the window. They both turned around. There was Will, pressing his nose against the glass, mashing it. Anything, Danny knew, to get a laugh. Anything and everything. "We gotta bounce," Will said. "Or we're going to get even more busted than we already are."

Danny nodded.

"You make the whole thing sound simple," he said to Tess.

"No, sir," she said. "From what you told me about this coach and the other players, it's going to be even harder than when you got cut that time. It's not Middletown now, it's not your dad's team, it's not all your friends cheering you on. But you *can* do this."

"Because you say I can?"

Tess put her hand out for a low five. When he didn't slap skin hard enough, she kept it out there, giving him a look, so he did it again, with more feeling this time.

"Now you're talking," she said, "like my Danny Walker."

Her Danny Walker.

Now she pulled him up out of his rocking chair, like a player helping him up after he'd gotten knocked down on the court, leaned down and gave him a quick hug before he knew what was happening.

"This one's for the championship of you, big guy," Tess said.

IT WAS TEN-THIRTY WHEN THEY STARTED BACK. WILL OFFERED TO help with the paddling this time, saying he didn't want to get ragged on for the whole rest of camp. But Ty said no, they needed to get back before breakfast.

Danny said, "What's the camp version of getting grounded for life?"

"Wait, I know that one," Will said. "You get more time with Coach Ed."

For some reason the trip back seemed to take twice as long to Danny, even though he was working just as hard with his paddle, still watching the way Ty did it, using his shoulders, bringing it back through the water until it was even with his hip, then lifting it straight up and doing the whole thing again.

Maybe, he thought, the whole thing felt like it was taking longer because he was moving away from Tess now instead of toward her.

Right before he had gotten into the canoe, he had asked her how long she was staying in Maine.

"I'm liking it better here already," she said.

"So you're going to hang around for a while?"

"Just to see how this all comes out."

Danny smiled, thinking about that part. Will must have been looking at him from where he was sitting in the middle of the canoe because he said, "Nobody should look as happy as you doing row, row, row your boat."

Danny told him to turn around and navigate. Will said they were doing fine on their own, but he'd keep his eyes peeled for icebergs so they didn't turn into Leo and what's-her-name in *Titanic*.

"Speaking of girls," Will said, "how'd it go with you and your conscience?"

"Tess is my friend, not my conscience," Danny said.

"*Girl*friend," Will said. "And conscience."

"She basically told me to stop acting like a total idiot," Danny said.

From the front of the canoe Ty said, "Sounds like a plan."

"She tells you to stop acting whack and you listen," Will said. "Is that basically it?"

"Basically."

Zach's head whipped back and forth as he tried to follow the conversation, like he was watching tennis. Beyond him, in the distance, Danny saw the lights from Right Way getting closer, started to wonder what the last part of their plan was going to be. It was, like, they'd busted out, now how did they bust back in without getting caught? His mom, the English teacher, always said the more books you read, the more you admired a good ending.

"Bottom line?" Will said to Zach. "He's always liked her better."

There was nobody waiting for them at the dock when they got there. Which meant that maybe nobody had come down there looking for them. Or, if they had, maybe they hadn't counted canoes. Or didn't know how many there were supposed to be in the first place.

Or, Danny thought, they knew one of the boats was gone and were just waiting for them back at their bunks.

He really didn't know what grounded for life meant at Right Way, just knew there was some kind of honor council made up of other campers. Mr. LeBow had told them about it the first day.

"If we do get busted—" Will said.

"*When* we get busted, you mean," Ty said, easing the canoe toward the side of the dock.

"—what are we going to tell them?" Will said.

"I'll handle it," Zach said.

They all looked at him. It was the first thing he'd said since they'd pulled away from Tess's dock.

"You'll handle it?" Danny said.

Zach was the one who smiled now. "If you're really staying," he said, "I got you."

With that, he stood up and, instead of jumping onto the dock, jumped into the water, just deep enough to be over his head. He swam ahead of them to the dock, hoisted himself up on the ladder at the end of it, stood there waiting for them in the moonlight, soaking wet.

"Like I told you," Zach said to Danny. "Wet."

It was when they came into the clearing between the woods and Gampel that they saw Nick Pinto and the counselor from Boston Garden, Bo Stanton, walking toward them with flashlights.

"Well, well, well, if it isn't the Lost Boys," Nick said.

Bo, who was about 6-6, had long black hair and a thin mustache. He was a senior forward at Boston College. "Or maybe just boys who think they're on *Lost,*" he said.

Nick, all business, said, "I assume you guys know the rules about leaving camp, day or night, without a permission slip, right?"

Before anybody else could say anything, Danny said, "It was my idea."

"And what idea was that, exactly?" Nick said. "You decide to leave by water?"

Danny couldn't decide whether Nick was mad about whatever he thought they'd done on the water, wherever they'd gone, or because of the whole deal with his knee the day before. "Listen, if you want to know the truth—"

"Then let me tell it," Zach said. "They didn't take the boat. I did."

They'd asked him on the dock why he'd jumped in the water. All Zach said was, "That's for me to know and for you guys to find out." Now here he was, taking a step forward, still soaking wet, looking like the biggest little stand-up dude at Right Way.

"Whoa, there, Danny Junior," Will said.

"Shut up for once and let somebody else talk," Zach said.

Danny said, "Zach, you don't have to do this."

"Yeah, I do."

Then he told Nick and Bo that some of the older kids had been picking on him earlier, threatening to stuff him in a locker. Nick asked which older kids, and Zach said he didn't want to squeal on them, he just wanted Nick to know how the whole thing started. "Anyway," Zach said, like this was something he'd been rehearsing inside his head, "I managed to get away from them—I may be small, but I'm fast—and hid down by the water. When it got dark, I snuck over to the canoes and took one out so I could be by myself."

"You took one of these out by yourself?" Nick said.

Zach grinned. "I'm a strong little sucker, too."

Tell me about it, Danny thought.

"Danny must have been worried about me," Zach said, "because he came down to the dock and saw me paddling away and he went and got these guys and they came after me."

Danny just waited now to see how Zach's version of a fish story would come out, like this was something he was telling around a campfire.

"How come only you and Walker are wet?" Nick said.

"I dropped my paddle," Zach said. "And when I dove in after it, Danny dove in after me, because he didn't know what kind of swimmer I was."

Zach looked up at Nick and Bo. "You can't punish them for trying to come after me," he said.

Nick said to the rest of them, "And you guys back him up on this?"

Nobody planned it, but they all stepped forward at the same time so they were even with Zach.

"Yeah," Danny said. "We've got his back."

At least that, he thought, *was the whole truth.*

And nothing but.

In the morning Nick said that he and Bo had talked it over after Danny and the guys had finally gone to bed and decided they weren't going to report them to Mr. LeBow.

"There's some holes in the little guy's story. You know that, right?" Nick said before leaving for breakfast.

Danny didn't say anything.

Nick smiled then. "I did the same thing one time, but there was a girl involved."

"She must have been worth it."

When Nick was gone, Danny waited for Zach to come out of the shower—he was one of the guys who actually did shower in the morning—and asked if he'd rather play basketball than eat.

Zach said, "You even have to ask?"

Zach grabbed his trusty ball, and Danny showed him the way

to a court set way off by itself, on the far side of the tennis courts, past the dirt parking lot they only used when parents came to visit the third weekend. Danny had found it the other day because he had heard a lot of noise coming from that direction on his way to the mess hall. The reason for the noise was that a bunch of counselors were using it for a street-style hockey game, tennis balls replacing pucks.

It was far and away the worst outdoor court at the camp, with a couple of holes near mid-court, and a net that was hanging by its last couple of strings.

But it was by itself, hardly any chance of anybody seeing them, unless a coach happened to come riding by in a golf cart.

"I'm skipping Froot Loops to play here?" Zach said. "And this is because . . . why?"

"You are a Froot Loop," Danny said, "coming up with a story like that in front of Pinto."

"It worked, didn't it?" Pride in his voice. A lot of pride. As if he'd earned some kind of merit badge last night. "I knew I had him when I gave him my sad face."

"I know the face," Danny said. "Remember?"

Zach was carrying his ball. Danny was carrying a broom he'd borrowed out of a storage closet at Gampel.

"Now that I see this court, I can see why you brought that," Zach said, pointing to the broom.

Danny took the ball from Zach, handed him the broom now.

"I've gotta sweep?" Zach said. "After I backed your play last night?"

"Backed my play?"

Zach looked embarrassed. "I always sound like a nerd when I try to talk like Tarik, don't I?"

"Don't worry, we all do," Danny said. He put his hand to his fist, like he was speaking into a walkie-talkie. "Calling all units," he said. "White boys trying to sound black."

"Yeah," Zach said.

"The broom's not for sweeping," Danny said. "It's for defense. I need you to be Ollie Grey."

"Ollie the shot catcher?"

"Him," Danny said. "Get over there and hold that sucker up, and I'll see how much space I need to shoot over it."

"My dad does this with me sometimes," Zach said.

"Mine, too." *He started doing this drill when he turned back into a dad*, Danny thought. *And when he started trying to turn me into him.*

"All dads do it for little guys," Danny said. "Or when they're trying to teach big guys to get more air under their shots."

He had Zach set up on the baseline, about ten feet from the basket to start. He told him to block any shot he could.

The first time Danny came dribbling hard from the right corner and pulled up, Zach swatted the shot into the grass. Like Will had that day at McFeeley.

"Sorry," Zach said.

"Don't be."

The next time, he came in, up-faked Zach while he still had his dribble, felt like he was shooting the ball as high as the backboard and watched it drop through the net.

"It's like one of Steve Nash's teardrop shots," Zach said.

"Yeah," Danny said, "except I want to use it to make big guys cry."

They stayed there an hour, switching off sometimes so that Danny had the broom—he told Zach that he might as well start putting this shot into his game now. No sad face on Zach now. Just determination.

Like looking in a mirror, Danny thought again.

"Were you really going to leave?" Zach said near the end, when they were taking their last break.

"Yeah," Danny said, "I was. I was going to do the same exact thing I told you not to do."

"And that girl changed your mind?" Zach said.

"No," he said, "she just made me see what a loser I'd be, and then I changed my own mind."

They went back one last time to the rim with the good net. Zach in the lane now, holding up the broom to Ollie height. Danny drove at him like he was driving to the basket, leaned in, stepped back, put up the teardrop again. The ball seemed to spend more time floating through the air than a kite.

And fell through.

Danny looked at Zach and made the sideways peace sign Tarik had shown them.

"He's baaack," Zach said.

"Not back," Danny said. "Just a little less whack."

THE REAL GAMES, THE LEAGUE GAMES, BEGAN LATER THAT DAY.

From now until the end of camp, they were scheduled to do only two clinics in the morning, have a one-hour practice with their teams after lunch, then play games all over the grounds starting at four o'clock.

According to the schedule posted outside The House, the Celtics' first game was at The House, against the Bulls.

"Aw, man, that's sick," Tarik said.

"Good sick or bad sick?" Will said.

"Bad," Tarik said. "They got two Brooklyn guys I played against in AAU last year."

Zach was with them, checking his own schedule. The younger kids played their league games at two-thirty.

"What's AAU?" he said.

"Amateur Athletic Union. Like travel basketball plus. In New York City, it's like the NBA of kids' ball. You make your chops in AAU. It means you're going places."

"Who are the Brooklyn guys?" Danny said.

"Kareem Dell is one," Tarik said. "TJ Tucker's the other. Both of them are fifteen, but they look like they're going on twenty. Both 6-3 already. Both got those long arms going for them. Both got ups."

"We talking ups like Ollie Grey the shot catcher?" Ty said.

"Dog," Tarik said, his voice sounding sadder than if his own dog had died. "Compared to them, Ollie jumps like Will here." He put his hand on Will's shoulder as he said the last part, before adding, "No offense, dude."

"My legs accept your apology," Will said.

"Well, that doesn't sound good," Danny said. "Not that it's going to matter much to me personally, if I'm not in the game."

"Hey," Zach said, "what about that new attitude you were telling me about?"

"That's right," Tarik said, raising his voice up to what he liked to call preacher level. "Don't be backslidin' on us now, baby. Don't be backslidin' now. Especially now that you got your lady across the lake."

Will, Ty and Zach had told Tarik the whole Tess story at lunch.

"My attitude's gonna be fine from now on," Danny said. "But it's like my dad always says, you gotta be realistic."

Kareem and TJ were as good as Tarik said they were. For the first half of the game, the Bulls coach, Tim Pedulla, from Hofstra—Danny knew him because Hofstra had nearly made the Final Four a few months before—seemed to run the same basic offense every time, the Bulls' guards pounding it inside on one side of the low post or the other, then watching as Kareem or TJ abused whatever big guys Coach Powers had guarding them, Ben Coltrane or David Upshaw or Alex Westphal.

Boys against men, Danny thought.

On the bench Tarik said to Danny, "First offense I ever saw with no weak side."

Just then, even with Rasheed dropping down and trying to help out, TJ Tucker faced up on David and got so high on his jump shot that Danny had this picture in his head that TJ had shrunk David to Zach Fox's size.

Danny and Will and Tarik didn't make much of a difference when they got out there in the middle of the first half. Danny thought he had played all right, a few assists, no turnovers, no shots attempted. But if it hadn't been for Rasheed getting hot right before halftime, the Bulls would have blown them right out of the gym already.

Bulls 40, Celtics 24 at the break.

They were playing sixteen-minute halves. Eight minutes into the second half, because Coach Pedulla went to his bench a little more, it was 52–42.

That's when Cole Duncan dove for a ball and went sliding into the bleachers like he was sliding into home.

Coach Pedulla got a butterfly bandage on the cut above Cole's eye, explaining that the skin on your forehead split pretty easily—it had happened to him a few times when he was playing.

Cole, who had started to cry when it happened—when a guy cried, especially in front of a bunch of other guys he didn't know, you knew he was hurt—was sitting up by then, holding an ice pack to his head, his eyes still red. He kept telling everybody he was fine, really he was. But they had already called for Dr. Bradley by then, who showed up and said he wanted to take Cole up to the infirmary. Just a precaution.

When Cole stood up, everybody on both teams started clapping. Then both coaches got their players back into the huddle. When the Celtics were around Coach Powers, he stared off into space for what felt like a long time, tilting his head to one side, then to the other, like he was having some kind of debate inside his head.

Finally, he turned and pointed at Tarik. "Get in there for Cole."

Danny, standing next to Tarik, saw him immediately bend one

leg behind him from the knee, then the other, a little stretching thing he did right before he went into the game.

"No," Coach Powers said now, "I meant Walker."

Danny was as surprised as any of them.

"Me?" he said.

"Is there another Walker on this team?"

"No sir."

"And let's mix it up a little once in a while," Coach Powers said. "Walker, you give Rasheed a break once in a while and play some point. Okay?"

Danny said he was good with that.

He didn't care how many plays he got to run. He was a point guard again, with the big boys this time.

Danny and Rasheed played as if they'd played together before, as if the game in North Carolina hadn't ended the way it did, as if Rasheed wasn't still hacked off about what he thought was Danny's flop, as if he hadn't leveled Danny just a couple of days before. It was as if he and Rasheed, for this one game, had thrown out everything except this:

Winning the game.

The Bulls were still bigger, but Kareem and TJ weren't making all their shots now, maybe because the guys up front for the Celtics—Ben, David, Alex—were playing bigger, fighting harder.

The rest of the time, Danny and Rasheed did their best, even in Coach Powers's offense, to turn it into a guards' game.

The way God intended, as Richie Walker liked to say.

With three minutes to go, it was 58 all. The Celtics weren't running every play the exact way Coach Powers wanted in practice, but they were moving the ball so well, passing it around so cleanly on just about every possession, that he didn't seem to mind.

Will came off the bench to make a three. Tarik was getting as many rebounds as anybody on their team. Danny lost count of how many jumpers Rasheed made to get them back into it. With half a minute left, the game was still tied, 64–64. Kareem Dell was at the line about to shoot the front end of a one-and-one.

Coach Powers called time-out.

"If he makes both, we run 'Carolina,' " he said. "If he misses the first, or makes the first and misses the second, run that variation of 'Carolina' where Rasheed comes down the baseline and curls around Tarik for a jumper."

Rasheed nodded, as if Coach Powers was really only running the play past him.

"Don't start it too late, Mr. Walker," Coach Powers said. "If they double or triple on Rasheed, he can throw it back to you. Put it on the floor like you're going to make a dribble drive, then get it back to him."

Danny clapped his hands together hard, answering him that way: Let's do this.

He wanted to show everybody how fired up he was, not even give them a hint at how tired he was. This wasn't clinic ball or scrimmage ball. This was real ball. The real thing. For the first time in a long time, being into every possession this way, every play, every pass, every shot. There were times when Danny was so into the game he was afraid to take a breath.

Until he was out of breath.

He saw Will looking at him in the huddle, like he knew. Just because he knew Danny could usually go all day in basketball without ever getting tired.

Wordlessly, Will handed Danny the plastic bottle of cold water he was about to drink himself.

Danny glanced at Rasheed now, who not only wasn't breathing

hard, he wasn't even sweating, as hot as it was in The House, even with the walls pulled back on the lakeside.

Kareem made the first free throw, missed the second, Tarik got the rebound, Danny came and got the ball. Bulls 65, Celtics 64.

Rasheed ran to the right corner, waited there. TJ Tucker was on that side and wasn't even watching his own man, Ben Coltrane. He was watching Rasheed. Danny was watching the clock. Twenty seconds now. Rasheed sprinted down the baseline, hand up, faking like he was waving for the ball. Tarik dropped down, set the pick where he was supposed to; Rasheed came around it.

Danny threw him the ball.

The guy guarding Rasheed was named Phil, Danny'd heard them call out his name a few times. He was Rasheed's size, blond and quick. Just not as quick as Rasheed. It was why Kareem Dell came over to help, TJ covering the lane behind him.

For the first time, Danny saw Rasheed Hill change expression.

He smiled.

Smiled like he was saying he still had the Bulls outnumbered, even if it was their two to his one.

He smiled and put the ball on the floor and did two lightning crossover dribbles—the double that made Danny's own double crossover look like something that belonged on training wheels. The move he used when he wanted to dust somebody and drive the ball to the basket.

Neither one of them bit.

Phil held his ground. So did Kareem.

Even Tarik's man came over.

Ten seconds now, and they had Rasheed surrounded.

He threw the ball back over to Danny, who'd been prepared to watch Rasheed win the game like everybody else.

He wasn't expecting to get the ball back, but managed to catch the pass at the top of the circle. Too far to even think about shooting it himself, if he was even thinking about it. But there was open space in front of him, the way Coach Powers imagined there would be if they sealed Rasheed.

Dribble drive, Coach had said.

Danny did, expecting TJ to come up. He didn't right away. Danny was a step inside the free throw line then.

Now TJ came up.

Out of the corner of his eye, he saw that everybody had stayed home on Rasheed, even as Rasheed was calling for the ball.

Pass or shoot?

Danny's only shot against TJ Tucker was the one he'd spent most of the morning practicing against Zach Fox.

The one over the broom.

Three seconds.

He planted his foot, stepped back just enough as TJ's right arm went straight up in the air, got the ball over him nice and high, making sure to keep his own right arm going straight at the basket to keep the shot on line.

A rainmaker of a shot if there ever was one.

Danny didn't hear anything, which meant that he'd gotten it off in plenty of time.

He watched it come down now.

About six inches short.

Air ball.

17

Rasheed didn't move when the horn sounded. He just stood there on the left wing until Danny looked over at him. Then Rasheed said, "I'm still open," before he turned and walked out the doors facing the lake.

Danny was about to go after him, apologize for losing the game, when he saw Coach Powers walking toward him from the bench area, gesturing for Danny to stay where he was.

"You did hear me say that even if he gave it to you after the first screen, you were supposed to give it right back," Coach Powers said. "Right?"

Danny looked down at this beautiful basketball floor, imagining up a hole for himself to crawl into. Knowing he was right back where he started with this coach, which meant in jail. "I didn't think there was time," Danny said.

"Too long an answer, son," he said. "All you needed to say was 'I didn't think' and leave it at that."

Then Coach Powers walked out of the gym in the exact same direction as Rasheed, as though they planned to meet up and talk more about how they gave Danny a chance to prove himself and how he'd screwed everything up.

"Yo," he heard from behind him.

Will.

Tarik was there with him.

"Before you say anything, I'm gonna say something, and it's that you played good," Will said. "And you know it. And the reason you know it is because you know more about basketball, and have more basketball in you, than that mean old man ever will."

"Scoreboard," Danny said in a small voice. Small as he felt.

Usually guys said that when they won. But to Danny, "scoreboard" always meant that however the game came out, that was the way it was supposed to come out.

"Wouldn't even have had a chance to win the game if you didn't play the way you did down the stretch, dog," Tarik said.

"I should have given it back," Danny said, not wanting to talk about this anymore, not wanting to be here anymore. "I don't agree with Coach about much. But the way Rasheed was going today, he could have made that J with his eyes closed, whether he had to rush it or not."

Will said, "Then maybe Rasheed shouldn't have given the ball up in the first place."

Then Will said they should go try to find Ty, maybe his game wasn't over yet and they could catch the end of it. Danny said, yeah, let's do it. Then he noticed the game ball sitting under the basket where somebody had left it.

Danny walked over, picked the ball up, dribbled out to the spot where he'd tried to shoot over Kareem. Like the hoop gods—his dad was always talking about the hoop gods, as though they watched every single game—were giving him a do-over. He dribbled in and shot the ball higher this time—nobody in his face, no long arms up in the air—and watched the ball drop through the basket.

Nothing but stinking net.

Then he jogged to catch up with Will and Tarik, wondering if those few minutes with Rasheed, before the air ball, was as good as it was going to get for him at the Right Way basketball camp.

. . .

It was Gampel's night to use the phone, which meant it was Danny's first chance to talk to his dad about everything that had—and hadn't—happened in the last day or so.

As soon as Richie Walker got on the line, he wanted to know everything about the knee, whether the swelling was on the inside or the outside, if the doctor was sure it was just a sprain and not ligaments, if the doctor was sure there was nothing floating around in there. His dad still considered himself a medical expert, not just on knees, but everything else after all the broken parts he'd had fixed in his life.

"Dad," Danny said, "I'm fine."

"Well, you're not fine if they still want to do an MRI," his dad said. "That doesn't sound fine to me."

Danny was in the phone booth with the door open, because it was a hot, muggy night in Cedarville. Zach was waiting to use the phone next. Danny closed the door now, even if Zach knew most of the story about the fake knee injury. It was more Danny being so embarrassed about what he was going to say next that he didn't even want *himself* to hear.

Like he was telling somebody he was afraid of the dark.

"When I say fine, Dad, it means I was never really hurt," he said. "I wanted an excuse to get out of here."

Out with it, just like that. He felt bad enough about having lied to the doctor and his mom and maybe himself. He was done with that, for good. He wasn't going to lie to his dad. Before he'd even considered doing something this lame, he should have thought about what his dad looked like in the hospital after his last accident. He should have remembered how his dad's basketball life—and nearly his whole life—ended in that first car accident his rookie year.

He could hear Tarik's voice inside his head now.

True *that*.

On the other end of the phone line, Richie Walker didn't say anything at first. It was one of those killer silences parents gave you sometimes, in person or over the phone, when they were trying to make you keep talking.

Or maybe his dad couldn't believe what he'd just heard.

"I'm not sure I heard you right," Richie Walker said.

Danny said, "You heard right."

Finally, Richie said, "That's not you." There was another pause and then he said, "Man, that's never been you."

"Dad," Danny said, "I know that now. I would have figured it out on my own. But Tess—she's here—got in my face the other night and made me see how dumb I'd been." He paused before he said, "Dad, believe me, there's nothing you could say that would make me feel worse than I already do."

"I don't care how much this coach got to you," Richie said. "You never fake an injury in sports. Never." He spit out the last word. "You quit before you do that."

"I know that now," Danny said.

"Do you?"

"Dad, I made a mistake, and I'm owning up to it. Isn't that what you always tell me to do?"

"You want a trophy for that?"

There was a lot more Danny wanted to tell his dad, to make him understand, wanted to tell him about Coach Powers saying he should switch sports, that maybe soccer would be better for him. But he was afraid it would come out sounding like one more lame excuse for faking the injury.

So he kept what had happened at Coach Powers's cabin to himself, through a silence from his dad that felt longer than eighth grade.

"You want to come home, come home," Richie said. "You want to stay, then show this coach he was wrong about you. Other than that, I've got nothin' right now. Talk to you soon."

Didn't say he loved him. Didn't wait for Danny to say that to him.

Just hung up.

Danny stood there, the receiver still to his ear, listening to the dial tone.

Then he took a deep breath, leaned out and asked Zach if he could make one more quick call. He pumped some change into the phone, called the number at Tess's uncle's house. He was going to tell her about the conversation with his dad, but when she came on, telling him in this happy excited voice about a fish she'd caught that afternoon, he decided against it. He would have skipped talking about the game, too, but she asked him about it once she was finished with her fish tale.

"Aren't you the one who always says there's a lot more that goes into a game than the last play?" Tess said.

"Yeah, but—"

Tess cut him off. "Forget the ending and think about the good stuff as a beginning."

"Okay," Danny said.

"Promise?"

It was a big deal with her, getting him to promise something.

"I promise," he said.

Danny wanted to know when he was going to get to see her again.

"I have my camera with me," she said. "Maybe my uncle can call Mr. LeBow and he'll let me come over to take some pictures."

"I'd be good with that," Danny said.

Tess said, "Until then, you can keep worrying about the way the game ended or suck it up and treat the good stuff like some kind of start."

"Are you trying to sound like my dad?"

"Your mom, actually," Tess said.

But at practice the next day it was as if the good stuff from the day before hadn't happened, at least as far as Danny was concerned.

Cole Duncan was back with Rasheed and the first unit, even with a bandage over his eye and a pretty impressive black-and-blue bruise showing around the bandage. Danny was with Will, Tarik, Alex Westphal and another forward, Tony Ryder, who'd missed the Bulls' game because of what Tarik and Will described as a truly epic night of hurling the night before.

On their way from practice to their four o'clock game against Lamar Parrish and the Lakers, Will and Tarik were still ragging on Coach Powers for the way he'd talked to them about what had happened against the Bulls.

"You listen to Dead Head Ed," Will said, "and Rasheed was going one-on-five when we came back on those suckers."

"Next year it's going to be 'Sheed saving the world on *24* instead of my man Jack Bauer," Tarik said.

It turned out to be a great game against the Lakers, even if Danny only played a quarter of it. The Celtics got ahead early because Rasheed couldn't miss and because their bigs, meaning David Upshaw and Ben Coltrane, were pretty much schooling the Lakers' bigs. And also because Lamar Parrish seemed to be making only about one of every three shots he took in the first half.

By halftime the Celtics were ahead by fifteen. Danny was hoping for a blowout, not just because he might get some extra minutes, but because he wanted to see Lamar Parrish suffer a little.

Or a lot.

But from the time the second half started, it was Lamar who couldn't miss. Didn't matter if Rasheed was on him or Cole. Or both. Didn't matter when the Celtics went to a zone, first a 3–2, then a box-and-one with Cole chasing. As much as Danny knew Lamar was a bad guy, it was like watching a pro take over a game.

Like watching the real Kobe.

With just over a minute left, he finally tied the game with a three-pointer. Danny was in the game now, because Will and Cole had both fouled out. Rasheed got fouled at the other end, made two free throws. Thirty seconds left. Celtics back up by two.

Wasn't enough.

Lamar calmly ran the clock down, drained another three, immediately ran to the other end of the court, holding the front of his jersey out, yelling "Uh huh . . . uh huh . . . uh huh."

Only the game wasn't over.

One second left.

As soon as the ball had gone through the net, Danny had turned to the nearest ref, calling one of the two time-outs he knew they had left, just because he always knew stuff like that. Then he ran over to Rasheed and said, "I know you don't like me, but you gotta listen to me, I've got a play that'll work. But you gotta tell Coach. He'll never take it from me."

As they walked toward their bench, he told him as fast as he could. When they got into the huddle, Rasheed laid out Danny's play for Coach Powers.

Coach Powers said, "You can make the pass?"

"Yeah," Danny said, "I can."

"What if they put somebody on the ball?"

"They haven't done that all day."

"You can make the pass?" Coach Powers said again.

"Yes."

Hoping he was right.

He took the ball at half-court. Alex screened Lamar the way he was supposed to. Danny fired the ball quarterback style, not at Lamar but directly at the backboard, as Rasheed came flying at the basket from the opposite side.

Danny's pass was right on the money, hitting the board right above the square, like a carom shot in pool, bouncing right into the hands of Rasheed Hill, who caught the ball and laid it in and won the game for the Celtics, 62–61.

As soon as the refs made the motion that it was a good basket, Lamar rushed the counselor working the clock. His coach and a couple of teammates saw what was happening, that Lamar was really going after the kid, and managed to cut him off. They finally got him calmed down enough to start moving him toward the door.

Before he was out the door he yelled over at Rasheed about winning the game with some tricked-up play.

Rasheed shrugged and actually smiled. "Not my play," he said. He nodded at Danny and said, "His."

Danny never showboated. His dad always said it wasn't in their blood. But he couldn't help himself, just this once. Now he smiled at Lamar, pulled his jersey out in front of himself, real fast, just once, and walked away.

"That's right, midget!" he heard from behind him. "Have your little fun now!"

"I think he's taking it well," Will said.

Danny had still felt like a spectator for most of the game. It was still Rasheed's team, the way the Lakers were Lamar's. The way the Warriors had been his team once. Here he was a role player, one who had come off the bench to help beat Lamar Parrish today. He was the kind of player who was going to get to shine like this once in a while, be expected to blend in the rest of the time.

He knew that was the way he had to approach things the rest of the way, do his best not to mess up, on or off the court, maybe even get another chance to make a hero play.

No such luck.

The very next day he was in Jeff LeBow's office. In the office and in trouble.

18

THE FIGHT STARTED WITH LAMAR TAKING ZACH'S BALL.

Danny had found Zach shooting by himself on a half-court nobody ever used on the woods side of Gampel. A lot of guys, as usual, were at the counselors' game, but Zach wasn't interested in watching the counselors play. If he could catch part of one of Danny's games, he would, just because it was Danny, because he'd use almost any excuse to hang around with Danny during the day, even though they were bunking together at night.

The rest of the time Zach Fox just wanted to go play.

The kid who'd showed up as the unhappiest camper at Right Way was happy as long as he had his ball and enough room to dribble and shoot it.

He was more interested in playing than he was in eating or sleeping or hanging with kids his own age. Danny still wasn't sure how much Zach loved camp. But as much as he still liked to complain about being here, he couldn't hide how much he loved basketball. Clinics, practices, games, it didn't matter. He was into it now. He had ended up on what sounded like the best team in the eleven- and twelve-year-old division. He liked his coach, an assistant from Northeastern University in Boston, a lot. Since that night when Danny had heard him crying himself to sleep, he had never said another word about leaving.

Zach was pretty much having the kind of camp Danny had been hoping to have, at least before Coach Powers came into his life.

On this night, he was working on his outside shot, something he'd turned into his summer job, shooting it correctly now, not launching it the way he had before he got to Right Way, the way Danny used to.

Danny was helping him, calling out pointers, mostly feeding him the ball, feeling like he owed Zach one for the day when Zach had stood there holding up that broom.

That's when Lamar came along.

Right away, Lamar started calling Zach Frodo, asking if he was practicing for the championship of Middle Earth, ignoring Danny at first, but clearly directing his insults at both of them.

Tarik would say later that he was surprised Lamar had even seen a *Lord of the Rings* movie. "Or understood it," Tarik said.

Zach tried to ignore Lamar, just kept shooting the ball.

But Lamar, being Lamar, wouldn't let up.

"How come you don't have those big Frodo feet?" he asked Zach. "Like you was wearin' Charlie Barkley's real sneakers, instead of those baby shoes you got on yourself?"

Now Danny said, "Leave him alone, Lamar."

Lamar looked at him. "What are you, his lucky charm? You do look a little like that leprechaun guy on the side of the box."

"Seriously, Lamar, you must have something better to do," Danny said.

"Listen to the boy beat me with his little tricked-up play. You still feelin' all puffed out about that?"

"I don't get puffed out," Danny said.

"I saw you after the game."

Danny couldn't help himself. "I was just trying to be more like you."

"You want to be more like me? *Grow,* little man."

"Let it go, Lamar."

Zach was still trying to pretend Lamar wasn't even there. So he took a couple of dribbles, shot the ball.

Big mistake.

Lamar went and got the rebound.

Looked at the ball and saw Zach's name written on it in Magic Marker.

"Your own little ball," Lamar said.

He bounced the ball a couple of times, then said, "Oh, looky here—it needs air."

Zach said it was fine the way it was, it had never needed air from the day he got it and could he have it back?

"No, midget," Lamar said. "I can always tell when a ball's flat, and this one is flat." Then he walked over to the little storage box that was at all the outdoor courts. Every box had pumps and needles inside, along with a bunch of indoor/outdoor balls.

"It's fine, really," Zach said.

"Can't a brother try to help?" Lamar said, a pump in his hands.

He stuck the needle into Zach's ball, pumped a couple of times, then smiled at Zach as he broke the needle off, knowing it was going to be stuck inside Zach's ball for good.

Every kid in the world knew what *that* meant.

The ball was ruined.

Forever.

Only then did Lamar Parrish give Zach his ball.

Zach stepped back and whipped it right at Lamar's head, the ball either catching Lamar on the side of his head or his shoulder, Danny couldn't tell for sure from the side. But wherever it hit, it made Lamar real mad, because he grabbed Zach by his shoulders and started shaking him, hard. Zach's head bounced around like he was a bobblehead doll.

Then Lamar lifted him up by his T-shirt, so the two of them were eye-to-eye for a moment.

Danny'd seen enough.

"Put him down, Lamar," he said, trying to sound calmer, more in control, than he really was.

Lamar, still holding Zach in midair even as Zach twisted and kicked his legs around, as if this took no effort on Lamar's part, laughed and said, "Right."

"I mean it," Danny said.

"He asked for it," Lamar said. "You doin' the same?"

"Guess so."

The last fight he'd gotten into, what he promised his mom and dad was the last fight he'd *ever* get into, was with a Middletown kid named Teddy (the Moron) Moran, who'd played for the other travel team in town, the Vikings, the team that had cut Danny. But Teddy was more mouth than anything else, more a threat to your ears than any other part of you.

Lamar Parrish was different. A whole lot different. A lot bigger than Teddy, a lot stronger.

A lot meaner.

"You want to pick on somebody, go back to picking on me," Danny said, not getting any closer. He didn't want it to look like he was trying to get up in Lamar's face, but he wasn't going anywhere, either. He felt his fists clench at his sides and hoped he wouldn't have to use them.

Because if he did, Lamar was going to use *his*.

Lamar put Zach down but kept a hand on him, the way you did on defense when you wanted to watch the ball and keep contact with the man you were guarding at the same time.

Zach said to Danny, "I can fight my own battles."

It made Lamar laugh. "Right," he said. "If you stand on the other Hobbit's shoulders, maybe." And then, in a move so fast Danny almost missed it, Lamar took his big right hand, the one he had on Zach, and flicked it into his stomach like a jab.

Zach Fox doubled over and sat down, gasping for breath, tears in his eyes.

Lamar looked down at him and said, "What are you, a girl?"

Without thinking, Danny charged Lamar then, lowering his shoulder and grabbing him around the waist, surprising him enough that they both went down.

Lamar rolled back up on his knees first, staring down at the dirt all over tonight's Kobe jersey, the purple road version, as though he couldn't believe what he was seeing. Then he looked down at the blood on the back of his right hand where he must have landed.

He looked at Danny, this crazed expression in his eyes and said, "This is *so* on, little man." Then: "Get up."

Danny did, not knowing what else to do under the circumstances.

He had no chance against this guy. He never should have gotten him madder than he already was, but he couldn't run away. Next to him he could hear Zach still choking for air, but he was afraid now to take his eyes off Lamar.

Who took a step now, like that quick first step he had in ball, drew back his bloody hand the way tennis players did when they were getting ready to hit a backhand.

Danny froze. Just stood there frozen and closed his eyes, waiting to get backhanded right across the court.

Only the blow never came.

"Get off me!"

When Danny opened his eyes, there was Rasheed Hill behind

Lamar, one arm around his waist, the other one with a pretty good choke hold around Lamar's neck.

"Get off me," he said again, weaker this time, because now he was the one who was having trouble getting enough air.

"Never cared for him much," Rasheed said to Danny. "Or his game."

" 'Sheed?" Lamar said in what voice he had.

"What?"

Lamar acted like he wanted to get loose, but Danny could see his heart wasn't really in it, not with the grip Rasheed had on his neck.

Lamar said, "You're takin' *his* side?"

"Yeah," Rasheed said, "I guess I am."

Lamar had gone into Jeff LeBow's office first while Danny and Zach and Rasheed waited outside. When he was finished, Jeff walked him out, to make sure there were no further incidents. It didn't stop Lamar from walking past them and saying "this ain't over" under his breath.

Now the three of them were in folding chairs set up across from Jeff's desk.

Principal's office, summer-camp version.

"Before any of you guys say anything," Jeff said, "you might as well know Lamar's side of the story. Basically, he says that Zach started it by whipping the ball at him, Danny blindsided him with what he called a block below the waist, then Rasheed jumped him from behind before those two counselors broke it up. There you have it."

Zach started to jump out of his chair, but Danny stuck out his arm, turning himself into a seat belt.

"Let me do the talking," he said to Zach.

To Jeff: "You're joking, right?"

"Do I look like I'm joking?"

"Mr. LeBow," Danny said, "that is, like, a total screaming *Liar, Liar*–like lie."

Zach couldn't restrain himself any longer, even if he did manage to stay in his chair. "He took my favorite ball away from me, one I brought from home, broke the needle in it on purpose—"

"He says it was an accident," Jeff said.

"—then he punched me in the stomach," Zach said, face red. "That's when Danny charged him."

"Listen, I know that Lamar can be a pain in the butt sometimes," Jeff said. "But he's the one with the bruised hand, and he's the one who was in the choke hold when my guys came by."

Now Rasheed spoke. "One he had coming to him."

"Three of you, one of him," Jeff LeBow said. "Just doing the math makes you guys look bad."

"Mr. LeBow," Danny said. "Do you think Zach or I would go looking for a fight with somebody Lamar's size?"

"Happens like this all the time in games," Rasheed said. "Guy hits you with a cheap shot, only the ref doesn't see that one. All he sees is when you go back at him."

"Then they make the only call they can," Jeff said.

Rasheed stood up now, pointed casually at Danny. "What he said happened, did. Do what you gotta do. I already did."

Then he walked out of the office.

The regular season at Right Way lasted fourteen games. There were eight teams in their league, so you played the other seven twice. The play-offs started the middle of the last week, which is when other college coaches and prep coaches from around the country showed up to scout.

Danny, Zach and Rasheed were suspended for two games each. In a short season like this, they all knew it was a lot.

Lamar got nothing. In the end, it was their word against his. Rasheed didn't help matters by saying if he wasn't worried about

171

breaking his hand, he wouldn't have just grabbed Lamar when he wound up to hit Danny, he would have dropped him.

In addition to getting the two games, Danny, Zach and Rasheed got two days of helping clean out the bathrooms in the bunkhouses while the afternoon games were going on.

"I don't even like going into those bathrooms when I *have* to," Zach said.

"It could've been worse," Danny said. "They could've kicked us out."

"Nothing's worse than cleaning toilets," Zach said. "Nothing."

It was the next morning before breakfast; they'd just been told their punishment in Jeff LeBow's office. He said they could participate in the morning clinics but weren't allowed to practice with their teams in the afternoon.

"That's when we'll be polishing toilets 'stead of our games," Rasheed said.

"I'm doing the showers," Zach said.

He went off to breakfast. Rasheed said he wasn't hungry, he was going to shoot around a little before clinics started. Danny asked if he wanted company, sure Rasheed would say no.

But to his surprise, Rasheed said, "Come along, if you want." Then he said he wanted to use the bad court by the parking lots. That way nobody would bother them.

Danny smiled, told him there was no such thing as a bad court as long as the rims had nets.

"Maybe in Middletown," Rasheed said. "Try coming to Baltimore sometime. Might change your mind."

The two of them cut around the main building, grabbed a ball somebody had left lying in the grass. Danny and the kid at camp he thought hated his guts the most.

When they got to the bad court they played some H-O-R-S-E, then a game of Around the World, then 21. When they got tired of games, they did something else Danny thought they'd never do.

Talked.

Rasheed said that most people never got past the way he looked, the hair and the tats. That's what he called them. Tats. Said that even though he was a kid, people looked at him and thought he was just like Allen Iverson. Or maybe some gangsta rapper who could play himself some ball.

"Do the tattoos hurt as much as guys say?" Danny said. "When you get them, I mean?"

Rasheed said you get used to it. He said his mom finally said he could get a few, but the deal was, he had to get As in school. Rasheed said he thought that was a fair trade. Danny pointed to one on his upper right arm that said "Artis" and asked who that was.

"My dad. He died when I was eight."

"Oh," Danny said, not knowing what else to say.

"He got shot."

Now Danny *really* didn't know what to say. He was afraid that if he asked how, he might find out something about Rasheed's dad he didn't want to know. Or be asking Rasheed to tell something he really didn't want to tell.

"Wasn't what you think," Rasheed said, as if he'd seen something on Danny's face. "He was in the wrong place at the wrong time, is all. Coming home from work one night when some guys from a couple blocks up decided to rob a liquor store and started shooting."

"I'm so sorry," Danny said, picturing it like some scene from a movie.

Rasheed said, "My mom says that's the big cause of death where we live, being in the wrong place at the wrong time."

They sat on a rock above the court, Rasheed telling Danny that basketball was going to be a way out of the neighborhood for him and his mom.

"Do people still call it the 'hood?" Danny said.

Rasheed almost smiled. "Only saltines from the suburbs."

"Saltines?"

"Little white guys from Middletown, USA."

"Hey," Danny said, "I didn't call it the 'hood, I was just sayin'."

Rasheed said he'd had chances to move, like to the school Lamar went off to, but that his mom had a good job working at a bakery, and she wanted him to go to Dunbar High, where his big brother had gone.

"That's where Sam Cassell went," Danny said.

"You know that?"

"Even saltines know stuff," Danny said.

Rasheed Hill turned and gave Danny some fist to bump.

"Your mom sounds cool," Danny said, thinking this was something else they had in common besides ball, cool moms.

"She's the one first told me that coming from a single-parent home wasn't some kind of death sentence," Rasheed said.

Danny wanted to say he'd been in a single-parent home for a long time when his dad was away but knew that he'd sound plain old stupid if he tried to compare his situation, his life, to Rasheed's. So he just fell back on the same thing he always did. "You want to shoot some more?"

"I'm good just chilling." Rasheed shook his head. "You believe we got two games and Lamar got nothin'?"

"You know," Danny said, "the first night I met you guys, I thought you and him were tight."

"That's what he wanted people to think, that me and him are boys. But we never were, even back in Baltimore. He just got with me that night walking back from dinner. I shouldn't have let him diss you down like that."

Now he really smiled. It caught Danny off balance, how happy it made him look.

"But I was still mad at you because you flopped," he said.

"Didn't flop," Danny said.

"You say."

"Because I didn't."

Rasheed put his thumbs together, stuck up his index fingers. The universal sign for "whatever."

"Now who's acting like a saltine?" Danny said. "But this isn't a whatever. If I say I didn't flop, I didn't." He stood up, fired up all of a sudden. "We gotta be clear on this if we're gonna be friends. If it's about basketball and I say something, you have to believe me. I got position, he made the call, I took the hit. If the ref had called it the other way, I would've had to accept it. Okay?"

Rasheed gave him that sleepy look and then said, "Okay."

They bumped fists again.

"Maybe," Rasheed said, "we're more alike than anybody'd ever think."

In the distance, they could hear the sound of Jeff LeBow talking into his bullhorn. At this time of the morning, it usually meant he was telling guys coming out of breakfast they had five minutes to get to their first clinic.

Danny got up, grabbed the ball from where it sat at Rasheed's feet, went out onto the bad court, bounced the ball between his legs, reached behind his back and caught it, bounced it through again without looking down.

Rasheed motioned for the ball. He spun it on his right index finger, rolled it down his arm, bent over so it rolled on his shoulders behind his head. The ball seemed to defy gravity as it went up his left arm until Rasheed was spinning it on the index finger of his left hand.

Danny felt like he was at the Globetrotters.

Finally Rasheed flipped the ball into the air, headed it into the air like a soccer player, watched along with Danny as it hit the backboard just right and went through the net, like he'd been practicing this shot his whole life.

"Let's get out of here," Rasheed said. "We're in enough trouble, we don't want to be late for clinics."

"I still owe you one for Lamar," Danny said as they cut back across the parking lot.

"Just play good when you get the chance," he said. "No way Lamar Parrish is gonna win the championship of this place."

"I don't play enough to make a difference."

"Not yet."

"Well, you must know something I don't."

"Not about basketball I don't," Rasheed said. He stopped and gave Danny the kind of shove guys gave each other sometimes. A good shove. "It comes to ball, you're just like me."

This time Danny knew what to say.

"Thank you."

"We're boys now," Rasheed said, and something about the way he said it let Danny know the conversation was over.

They walked across one parking lot, then another, Danny dribbling the ball for a while, then handing it to Rasheed, letting him dribble it, back and forth that way until they were back in the middle of the morning action at Right Way.

Him and Rasheed.

Boys now.

THE CELTICS LOST BOTH GAMES THEY PLAYED WHILE RASHEED AND Danny were in the penalty box, which is how Rasheed described the bathrooms they had to clean.

The two losses did nothing to improve their coach's already crabby disposition. So even when they returned to practice, Coach Powers was still fixed on what had happened with Lamar that night and how it had cost the whole team.

How Danny had cost the whole team.

Coach Powers: "Because Mr. Walker here dragged Rasheed into his little drama, we have now lost two games and fallen to the bottom of our division and are on our way to having a bad seeding when the play-offs start."

Rasheed stepped out of the line, saying, "But, Coach, I thought I explained to you—"

Danny got in front of him before he could say anything else.

He wasn't going to let Rasheed fight his fight every day.

"It's all my fault, definitely," Danny said. "You're right, if I hadn't interfered in the first place, Rasheed wouldn't have had to."

"You should have thought of that two days ago," Coach Powers said. "But there's no point beating a dead horse."

When they got on the court, Tarik whispered to Danny, "Usually the man don't stop beatin' the horse till it's already at the danged glue factory."

Their game later that afternoon was on one of the outside

courts, against the Nets. Rasheed dominated from start to finish, as if all the ball he'd kept inside of him for the last two days just exploded out of him. And Tarik had his best game by far, twelve points and twelve rebounds.

Danny played his usual one quarter, down to the second. But on this day he might as well have not played at all, because he was afraid to make any kind of mistake and get his coach any madder at him than he already was. He didn't take a single shot or make a single pass that anybody would have remembered. Was basically just out there, especially in the second half, when the Celtics were running off as much clock as possible by way of protecting the big lead they'd piled up in the first half.

On this day, he was back to being Mr. Spare Part.

It was after the game, when they were sitting on the grass while Coach Powers wore them out telling them what he'd liked in the game and what he hadn't, that Rasheed informed them all that he thought he might have tweaked his hamstring and might not be able to play tomorrow.

Coach Powers said for him to go ice it—it would probably feel a lot better in the morning.

Rasheed said he wasn't so sure and made a face as he stood up. Danny tried to remember when he might have hurt himself. But all he'd seen, all day long, was another game when Rasheed seemed to be playing at a different speed than everybody else, in a different league, even though the Nets had come into the game with the second-best record in the division.

"Don't want to take any chances, is all," he said to Coach Powers. "I try to force it tomorrow and make it worse, I could end up missing the play-offs."

Coach Powers said they sure wouldn't want that to happen,

then reminded him about the ice. By now everybody on the team knew that in Ed Powers's world, ice could cure everything except chicken pox.

Rasheed left the court with Danny, Tarik and Will. Like the four of them had been hanging all along. *Being friends with somebody can seem like the hardest thing going*, Danny thought, *until it feels like the easiest thing in the world.*

"When *did* your leg start acting up on you, dog?" Tarik said.

"Didn't."

"But you said—"

"Know what I *said*," Rasheed said. "It's just not exactly the same as what *is*."

"I'm confused," Will said.

Tarik grinned. "Tell me about it."

"I mean about Rasheed," Will said. To Rasheed he said, "Are you hurt or not?"

"I felt a little something pull when I lifted Lamar up off the ground," he said. "That much is the truth. But it's not so bad that I can't play."

"But you told Coach you're not playing," Tarik said.

"I'm not," Rasheed said, then nodded at Danny. "He is."

"You're not taking a day off because of me," Danny said. "Uh-uh. No way."

"Way," Rasheed said. "I'm not just doing it for you. I'm doing it for the team."

"Okay," Will said, "now I really don't get it."

"We're never gonna be as good as we're supposed to be if Walker doesn't play more," he said. "You'd think that man would have got past himself and figured that out by now. But he hasn't. So now I'm gonna help him out a little."

Tarik said, "The way you'd help some real old person cross the street. Along the lines of that."

"Yeah," Rasheed said. "Along the lines of that."

Danny was on his way to the game the next day when he saw Lamar Parrish talking to Tess. She'd said she was going to just show up one day and surprise them, take a few pictures. Danny had only thought it was a good idea because it meant he got to see her again before she left.

Now here she was.

With Lamar.

Surprise! Danny thought.

There was nobody else around. It was just the two of them, in the middle of the great lawn at Right Way, where Jeff had greeted everybody the first day of camp.

There was a big old tree outside Jeff's office, and Danny stepped back to let it hide him, trying to decide whether to go over there or not, find out for himself what was going on.

He had managed to stay out of Lamar's way since the fight. Actually, he and Zach and Rasheed had been ordered to steer clear of Lamar until the end of camp. But Danny didn't need to be told that by Mr. LeBow or anybody else. He knew that if something else happened he'd only get blamed all over again. Or get kicked out of here. And even though that was something he had wanted to happen a few days ago, when he'd tried to weasel his way home, things had changed.

He'd promised himself he was going to stick it out. Get something out of these three weeks. It was like when you set your mind on getting a good grade in a class you stunk at, or just plain hated. He was going to do it, no matter what. A promise was a promise, even if it was one you made to yourself.

Only now there Lamar was with Tess.

Tess.

She didn't look as if he was bothering her, but that didn't mean anything. Maybe he just hadn't bothered her yet.

Should he go over or not?

Danny saw Tess hand Lamar her camera.

That's what happened across the lawn, anyway. Inside Danny's head, he couldn't help it, he saw Lamar taking Zach Fox's basketball.

That's when he came out from behind the tree, walking over there as fast as he could without it looking like he was running, like this was Danny to the rescue all over again.

"Hey," he said, trying to make himself sound casual when he got to them. "What's doin'?"

"Hey, yourself," Tess said. She smiled at Danny, the way she always did when she saw him, at school or at a game or just walking down the street in Middletown.

As nervous as he was, he smiled back. Then gave a quick look at Lamar, who was smiling himself. Only not because he was as happy to see Danny as Tess Hewitt was.

To Tess he said, "You're the one."

"Excuse me?" she said.

Lamar was nodding now, saying, "The one we all heard about the night him and his boys took the boat. His girl from back home."

Danny wasn't going to get into it with Lamar Parrish, of all people, about whether Tess was "his" girl or not.

Tess poked Danny and said, "Thanks for making me famous."

Danny said, "So what're you guys doing?"

"Lamar wanted to take a look at my camera," Tess said. "He's interested in photography."

Danny wanted to say: Yeah, but only if somebody's taking a picture of *him*.

"Cool," Danny said, though feeling decidedly uncool at the moment, just wanting to get Tess away from this guy.

But Lamar seemed in no hurry to go anywhere.

He said to Tess, "Sure is a fine piece of equipment you got here."

Now he turned and smiled at Danny, winked at him as he held Tess's camera high in the air, as if wanting to study it from all angles. "Yeah, no doubt, a fine piece of picture-taking equipment. Probably takes pictures a lot better than my cell phone."

He was really playing with Danny now. They both knew it. Tess was too smart not to see it, too, hear it in his voice. Maybe that was why she put her hand out, like she wanted her camera back, and said, "Well, I've got to take off. I want to get some pictures of the other Middletown guys as long as I'm here."

"I hear that," Lamar said, and started to hand the camera back to her. "I gotta bounce, too. Almost game time."

But as he started to hand over the camera, he fumbled it, like you did when you were playing Hot Potato, fumbled it like he was about to drop it.

Danny lunged and got his hands underneath it, the way you did when you tried to keep a ball from hitting the ground.

Lamar was just teasing them.

"No worries, little man," he said. "I got it."

He handed the camera back to Tess, gave her a small bow, said "nice talkin' at you" to her, ignoring Danny again. Then he left, walked away from them in the slouchy way he had, bopping his head, swaying a little from side to side, as though he knew they were watching him, as though he was the most awesome person in this whole camp.

"Well," Tess said, "that certainly weirded me out."

"That," Danny said, "was just Lamar being Lamar. Wanting me to know that he knows about us."

Tess smiled. "Us?"

Danny could feel himself blushing, so he looked away, like he was still trying to track Lamar. "Us being friends," he said. "You know what I meant."

"Always," Tess said.

"You ought to stay away from that guy," Danny said. "Everything that just happened, probably even talking to you in the first place, was for my benefit. There's something about me that makes him want to push my buttons. And I have a feeling it's going to get worse now that he sees Rasheed hanging around with me."

"Don't worry, big fella. I can take care of myself," Tess said. She slung her camera bag over her shoulder and looked like a total pro to Danny as she did. Danny knew how much she loved that camera, a gift from her parents last Christmas, probably her prize possession. It was why he had lunged for it the way he had. "You just worry about playing ball."

Now, she said, she was going off to take some pictures, since this was her one afternoon to do that, and her uncle was picking her up at dinnertime. She asked Danny where his game was and he said Court 4, then asked where Ty was playing, and Danny told her that, too.

"If you see Lamar, head in the other direction," Danny said. "That's my new policy."

"If I see him again, I'll tell him not to mess with Tess," she said, and laughed at her rhyme. Then she headed off across the lawn on those long legs, looking as if she didn't have a care in the world.

All these hotshot players at this camp, so many of them as stuck on themselves as Lamar was, and for this one day a girl was the most awesome person here.

Maybe it was seeing Tess right before the game, Tess who wasn't afraid of anything or anybody, that gave him the right kind of attitude adjustment. Whatever it was, he played his best game yet.

By far.

Even though Rasheed had said that Coach Powers would start him, Danny didn't believe it until it happened, until he was told right before the game against the Nuggets that it was going to be him and Cole in the backcourt. "They've got a couple of guys in the backcourt almost as small as you," Coach Powers said. "You and Cole should be able to handle them."

He told Cole to handle the ball. But in the first five minutes, Coach Powers could see what everybody else could, that the little guy guarding Cole was giving him fits, picking him up full-court, making him struggle just to advance the ball past half-court, much less get them into their offense.

They were down twelve when Coach Ed called a time-out and told Danny to go to the point.

"Your ball," Rasheed whispered to Danny when they broke the huddle.

Danny knew Coach was only turning the team over to him this way as some kind of last resort. He didn't care. He wasn't going to overanalyze everything this time, especially if this was going to be the one start he got in Maine. He was just going to let it rip, the way he had when it had been him and Rasheed together in the backcourt.

That was exactly what he did.

He started breaking down the dark-haired kid guarding him off the dribble, getting into the lane, feeding Ben Coltrane and David

Upshaw for easy buckets, even though both Ben and David had bigger guys guarding them. The dark-haired kid tried to press him all over the court, and Danny made him pay, even after made baskets, making it seem as if the Celtics were constantly on the break. The Nuggets coach—Tarik said he was from Manhattan College—switched Cole's guy over on him and that didn't help, either. Danny would keep pounding it inside or kicking it out to Will, who on this day was making threes as if he were back at McFeeley Park.

Today Danny played ball as if he still had the eye.

He played as if it was travel team all over again.

The Celtics got the lead by halftime. But the Nuggets hung in there in the second half, mostly because of their size advantage. Before long, the game was going back and forth, one lead change after another. Nobody had more than a three-point lead in the second half. One of those games. For once, even Coach Powers got out of the way and let them play. He still called out plays, just not every time down the court.

Ben Coltrane fouled out. The Celtics hung in, even with Tarik playing center now. David Upshaw fouled out. Still they hung in. Then Alex Westphal, their last real big guy, fouled out. They were going with four guards now, plus Tarik.

They were down two points with twenty seconds left when Coach Powers called their last time-out.

"Quick two and a stop," he said.

Quick two and a stop, Danny knew, meant overtime. Tarik had four fouls. When he was gone, it would look like the Nuggets were playing Zach's team.

Their best chance was to win now.

"But Coach—"

That was as far as Danny got. Coach Powers glared away the rest of the thought.

"Cole, you set a back screen for Tarik," he said. "Then go to a zone at the other end, pack it in, make them take the last shot from the outside. When they miss—and notice I said *when*—we'll get 'em in overtime."

Danny nodded as if he agreed, as if this was the best idea anybody had ever had.

Only he didn't agree. Will was on fire, and Danny knew their best chance was to win the game right here.

The five in the game joined hands before breaking the huddle. As they did, Danny made eye contact with Rasheed, who was behind Coach Powers, shaking his head no, holding up three fingers, as if he'd channeled himself right into Danny's brain.

Now Danny was sure he was right. This was Will's day, too, his chance to show Coach he was wrong about him, same as it was Danny's. Will's chance to do something he hardly ever got to do in basketball:

Make the hero shot and win the game.

But he had to make the shot. If he didn't, if Danny busted the play, and then Will missed, and the Celtics lost their third in a row, Coach Powers would banish Danny to the end of the bench once and for all.

On the way out of the huddle, he said to Tarik, "Do me a favor?"

"Whatever you need," Tarik said. "You've been makin' me look like a star today."

"Don't get open," Danny said. "Even if it means you don't get to take the last shot."

Tarik smiled. "We gonna roll the dice with the funny man, right?"

"You got it," Danny said. Then quickly told him the play they were going to run after they didn't run Coach Powers's play, right before he went over and told Will.

Cole set the back screen the way he'd been told, and it was a good one. Only Tarik cut the wrong way coming around it, giving his man a chance to pick him up.

Everybody was still covered.

There were still fifteen seconds left. All day. Danny looked over at Will and nodded. Telling him to make his move. The play was "Ohio." A play they used to run all the time with the Warriors in travel. Will would run from the left corner to the right corner, Tarik screening for him right under the basket as Will blew past him.

It worked the way it always had, and Danny, still with his dribble, saw Will break into the clear.

He threw the pass before Will even got to his spot behind the three-point line, fired this high pass over the top of the defense that must have looked like it was headed for the next court over.

Threw it to the spot the way quarterbacks did before the receiver even made his cut.

The kind of pass you threw if you still had the eye.

Will had to jump to catch the ball. But he caught it cleanly, came down with it as his man, this stocky kid with a buzz cut, came tearing at him. The buzz-cut kid was a step late as Will squared his shoulders and let the ball go, and the only reason he didn't see that it was money all the way was because the buzz-cut kid was blocking his view.

Celtics 51, Nuggets 50.

"I am so wet," Will said when Danny got to him, "my name should be Free Willie Stoddard."

All around them, the whole team was happy, like they were finally one team, even on a day when their best player had been sitting next to the coach. Rasheed, forgetting he was supposed to have a sore leg, hugged Will and lifted him off the ground the way he had Lamar that night, only in a good way this time. They were all high-fiving each other and then a few of them were in this pig pile on the court. Danny thought about diving on top, but then he just walked up to Tarik, jumped as high as he could, and chest-bumped him.

"Needs work, dog," Tarik said.

It was then that Danny noticed Coach Powers sitting in the same folding chair he'd sat in during the game, calmly motioning for Danny to come over.

Danny jogged to him.

"You ran your own play, didn't you?" Coach Powers said.

Danny looked off, to where the happy part of the team still was. "Yes."

No more lies.

Coach Powers didn't say anything right away, just got slowly up out of his chair, stood there towering over Danny until he said in his quiet voice, "Next year tell your father to send you to a camp where the boys get to coach the teams."

Even when I win here, Danny thought, *I lose.*

21

THEY WERE ALL AT THE END OF ONE OF THE LONG PICNIC-BENCH TA-
bles, about two minutes into dinner, when Tess showed up.

Danny, Will, Ty, Tarik, Rasheed, Zach Fox: They were all there,
ready to consume a record amount of camp pizza, planning the
game of Texas Hold 'Em they were going to play later using poker
chips Will had brought.

Then Tess was there, camera bag over her shoulder. She barely
got out the words.

"Someone broke my camera!"

The girl who could handle herself in any situation was crying.

Will jumped up right away, sensing everybody in the mess hall
was watching them and probably wondering what a girl was doing
there. "Let's take this outside," he said, and started walking Tess
toward the door.

The rest of them followed her, not worrying about pizza night
anymore, just wanting to get Tess outside as fast as they could.
Keeping her in the middle of them as they walked out the door and
around the corner, past the main building and out onto the lawn,
not too far from where Danny had seen Tess with Lamar.

Lamar: Talking about what a fine piece of equipment Tess's
camera was, then giving Danny that look.

"It was all my fault," Tess said.

"Somehow I doubt that," Will said.

Danny just kept staring at Tess, wanting to say or do something that would make her feel better. Her eyes were red, and there were those pink dots she got when she was upset, not just making her look sad, making her look younger. Tess Hewitt, who always looked, and acted, older than everybody else, certainly any guys she was hanging around with.

Who never cried in front of Danny or anybody else.

He stared at her and thought back now to how close she'd come that day at McFeeley. He felt more sure than ever that he was never going to be mean to her ever again if he could help it.

"What happened?" Danny said to her. "From the beginning."

She took her bag off her shoulder and removed what was left of her prized camera, which looked as if it had been dropped out of a high window.

Or run over.

"This happened," she said.

"We know," Danny said. "What we want to know is how."

She said that she'd shot some pictures of Danny's game, then decided to wander around for a little while, taking random shots for fun, finally stopping at a pickup game some older kids were playing at the court in front of Staples.

Her uncle had left her a text message on her cell phone saying he was going to be a little late picking her up in his boat, so when she heard the dinner horn sound, she figured she'd come find them and say good-bye before she walked down to the dock. So she headed up toward the mess hall. On her way, she ran into Mr. LeBow, who was going to dinner himself. She asked if there was a ladies' room she could use. He showed her the one next to Sue's office, on the other side of the main building, near the back door.

"I dropped my bag outside," Tess said. "You know, the way you drop your backpack at school."

She said she was in there for five minutes, tops, just washing up at the end of a day when she'd felt as sweaty as the players.

When she came back out, the camera was out of the bag, lying on the ground, looking the way it did now.

"Who'd do something like this?" she said, eyes big again, starting to fill up.

"Lamar, that's who," Danny said.

"True that," Will said. "Danny told us he was messing with the camera before."

Ty said, "Was he in that pickup game you talked about?"

"No," Tess said. "He was at the next court over, shooting around by himself."

"Figures," Tarik said.

"I need to go ask him something," Danny said, and took one step before Will and Ty blocked his way. Both of them had their arms crossed.

Shaking their heads no.

"Bad idea," Will said.

"The worst," Ty said.

"But he did this. He's got it in for me now, and you guys know it."

"We got no proof," Rasheed said.

"We only got what we think we got," Tarik said.

"You know," Will said, "if this were TV, we could have them dust Tess's camera for fingerprints."

"Dog," Tarik said, "you watch way too much of that dang *CSI*."

Danny asked Tess if there was anyone else around when she discovered what had happened to her camera. She said no. Did she report it to anybody? No again. "I did the only thing I could think of," she said. "I came looking for you guys."

"We gotta find Lamar and at least put it to him!" Danny said now. "Ask him why he'd do something to somebody who has nothing to do with any of this."

"Well, nothing 'cept you," Tarik said.

When Danny finally calmed down, it was decided they would go tell Mr. LeBow what happened. Only, when they got over to his office, it was locked up, probably for the night. So they got some paper out of the computer room, and Danny wrote a short note, trying to make his handwriting readable for once, telling Mr. LeBow what had happened, not putting anything in there about Lamar, just saying they'd tell him the rest of the story in the morning. Saying in the note that Tess was at camp for just this one day taking pictures and that whoever did this to her shouldn't be allowed to get away with it.

Then Tess asked Danny if she'd walk him to the dock.

He reached up without saying anything and took the camera bag off her shoulder, surprised at how heavy it was.

There was nobody on the beach, maybe because it had gotten cold all of a sudden, like the total opposite of the day. It was darker than it should have been at eight o'clock in the summer, probably because of the storm predicted for later that night.

"I loved that stupid camera," she said.

"I know."

"When I called my uncle, he said he'd drive me to Portland tomorrow. There's a great camera store there," Tess said.

"So you'll get a new one."

"It just won't be this one."

He saw the pink dots reappear on her face, saw her eyes getting big again. But then Tess gave a quick shake of her head, like she was telling herself that she was done crying, at least for tonight.

"You're sure it was Lamar," she said.

"I'm sure."

"It's got to be more than him just wanting to get at you through me," she said. "Doesn't it?"

She really wanted to figure this out, understand it. By now, Danny knew Tess was curious about everything, even Incredibly Dumb Guy Stuff.

"He's a bully," was the best Danny could do. "Bullies do stuff like this because they can. They do it even if they're as good at something as Lamar is at basketball. Heck, you see it all the time in pro sports." Smiling now as he heard himself say that to her. "Well, *you* don't, but I do. Guys like Lamar get away with everything until teams finally decide they're not worth the trouble. And even after that," Danny said, "they usually get a few last chances."

"That doesn't make it right."

"It's not right," Danny said. "It's just sports."

"But that's not the way it is with you in sports," she said. "Or Will or Ty or Tarik or even Rasheed."

"Nope," he said, "you're right about that. Maybe most right about Rasheed, even if he's the one of us you know the least. He told me that people can't get past his looks, and maybe I couldn't either, at least at the start. But it turns out he's more old school than I am."

"Impossible," she said. "Whatever the oldest school in the world is, you're older than that."

They heard two sounds, one after another. First, thunder in the distance, then the sound of the boat. Danny swiveled his head around and saw the floating water bed heading their way, Tess's uncle behind the wheel.

Danny handed Tess her camera bag and as he did, like it was all one motion, he got up on his tiptoes and gave her a hug. It didn't last long. But it was definitely a hug.

When he pulled back he said, "You okay for real?"

"I will be tomorrow," she said, then pointed a finger at him. "And remember. No going looking for Lamar tonight. No payback. No more trouble. Promise?"

He nodded.

"Say it, mister."

"I promise."

She told him he didn't have to walk her the rest of the way, ran down toward the boat and tossed her bag to her uncle, no longer having to worry about damaging what was inside. Her uncle reached up to take her hand. As he did, Tess turned around and shouted to Danny at the other end of the dock.

"Do not even think about losing to that guy," she said.

They both knew who she meant.

"Got it," he said.

I just hope we get the chance in the play-offs, he thought.

And if we do, I just hope I get my *chance.*

The rain started as the boat pulled away from the dock, and within about a minute was coming down hard. Danny ran up the hill, wondering if the guys might still be playing cards. But he didn't feel like cards tonight. He decided to go back to Gampel instead, read one of the actual books he'd brought with him to camp, an old-time book his dad had given him called *Championship Ball,* about a guy his dad always referred to as Chip Hilton, All-America. "When it comes to basketball," Richie Walker said, "Chip Hilton, All-America, is just like you, only taller."

Danny came out of the woods and took a hard right toward Gampel, walking now. There was no point in running—he was already soaking wet, the rain had become a storm that fast.

He was about fifty yards from Gampel when he saw Lamar standing alone in the rain between Danny and the front door, not wearing a Kobe jersey on this night, wearing a purple Lakers hoody instead, smiling at Danny like he'd been waiting for him.

Great.

Danny just put his head down and kept walking, remembering what he'd just said to Tess about no trouble. Even if trouble was standing right there in front of him.

Lamar, in a voice loud enough to be heard over the wind and rain, said, "Too bad there about your girl's camera."

Danny didn't think Lamar would try anything. There were other kids all around, coming from different directions, running for shelter. So he just kept moving, thinking as he did about an expression his mom liked to use in class when one kid would say he'd only gotten into a beef because another kid was bothering him or her.

Next time, she'd say, do not engage.

"The things people do to other people's property," Lamar said. "It's just a dang shame."

Danny was past him now, not wanting to run, almost to the door.

"What?" Lamar said from behind him. "You don't want to talk to me tonight?"

Do not engage.

Danny was at the door now, starting to turn the handle. He was that close to being inside and out of the rain and away from the sound of Lamar Parrish, who wanted to trash talk you even in the middle of a rainstorm.

Danny turned around, not even sure why, looked right at Lamar, smiled at him now.

"Hey, Lamar," he said.

"S'up, midget?"

Danny dribbled an imaginary ball, made a motion like he was shooting his new jump shot, showing him that perfect form he was working on, like he was putting one up over Lamar from the outside. When he was done, he held the pose in a way he never would in a game, right arm still high, the way Michael Jordan held the pose the night he made the shot in the Finals to beat the Utah Jazz that time.

As if the imaginary shot Danny'd just taken was money all the way.

Now he walked into Gampel, not waiting to hear what else Lamar had to say, not caring, closing the door behind him, thinking to himself, *That's the way I want camp to end.*

At least in my dreams.

22

LAMAR GOT AWAY WITH IT, OF COURSE.

"No nothin' for a know-nothin'," is the way Tarik described it.

When Jeff LeBow asked about Tess's camera, Lamar just said he shot baskets right up until he went to dinner with some of the guys from the Lakers and that if Mr. LeBow didn't believe him, he should go right ahead and ask them. Then he acted hurt that Mr. LeBow would even think to ask him about something like that, saying, "If I'm gonna be a suspect for every little thing that happens from now to the end of camp, maybe I should make a call to Hoop Stars right now, see if they still want me."

Hoop Stars was an equally famous, competing camp in western Pennsylvania, Danny knew by now, fighting Right Way for the best players every summer, even though Hoop Stars started a couple of weeks later.

"Fortunately, I got him calmed down," Jeff said.

Wow, Danny thought, *what a relief.*

This was after lunch the next day. Danny was in his office, and Jeff was describing his meeting with Lamar, actually trying to tell them how much Lamar liked meeting Tess, how he was hoping to get what he called some Kodak-taking tips from her if she showed up again, just so he could have his own pictures to take home to his mom.

Knowing he was wasting his time, Danny said, "He did it."

"If you don't stop saying things like that," Jeff said, "I'm going to end up breaking up a fight a day between you guys."

"I'm not looking to fight him," Danny said. "I can see now that he's going to win any kind of fight between us." Then he paused just slightly before saying, "except maybe on the court."

"What do you want?"

"For you to see him for what he really is, I guess."

"And what's that?"

"Another guy in sports who's a great player and a bad guy."

"I'm just a guy running a basketball camp," Jeff said. "Josh Cameron's camp. A camp Mr. Cameron is going to be showing up at any day now. And when he does, I'd prefer that he doesn't think the whole thing has turned into *Meatballs* or one of those other dumb camp movies. You say you want to beat him on the court, so wait and beat him on the court."

Danny said he'd try and left.

He was trying. His dad called it grinding. That morning he and Ty had gotten up early and worked out on the bad court, just the two of them, for an hour. Danny had worked more on defense than offense, knowing that one of the ways to get more minutes from Coach Powers in the games he had left was to show he could handle bigger guys, that when other teams tried to use his size against him—gee, that had never happened before—he wasn't going to give up easy baskets.

So they played one-on-one, and Danny told Ty to post up on him as much as he wanted, kept stopping the game to ask what he was trying to do on every play, what worked against that particular move and what didn't.

Ty said that what he concentrated on the hardest when he had a mismatch was to *not* bring the ball down. "Like coaches always say," Ty said. "Bring the ball down, and you turn a big guy into a little guy."

Danny said, "I wish it were that simple."

Eight in the morning and it was so hot already they were sweating buckets. "Coach Rossi talks about it every day," Ty said. "He says, anytime that ball comes down, it's ours."

So they worked on that. Your natural reaction on defense was to put your hands up when a guy was getting ready to shoot. But the key was making your move right before that, reading the guy, keeping your hands out in front of you, ready to flick at the ball or snatch at it as the guy went from his dribble into his shot.

Even against somebody as smart and good and long as Ty, Danny started to get the hang of it, getting his hands on the ball a surprising amount of the time. Every time he did, Danny told Ty not to make it easy for him. And every time he said that, Ty said he wasn't making it easy, Danny was actually starting to annoy him.

It was a good thing, they both decided, even if the long-range plan was annoying another guy Ty's size.

One who liked to go around in a Kobe jersey.

The Celtics were 6–6 with two games to play.

Danny was up to playing two quarters, without knowing if it was because Coach Powers thought he was improving or just because Rasheed was working on the coach every chance he got. But Danny was getting more of a chance, even when games were close in the fourth quarter.

The Celtics weren't the best team here, and Danny had seen them all by now. The two best teams were Ty's team, the Cavaliers, and Lamar's Lakers. That didn't mean the Celtics couldn't beat them in a one-game season. But in his heart—that old thing—he knew that could only happen if it was him and Rasheed in the backcourt, and not just for a handful of minutes a game.

Nothing against Cole. Danny liked him as a kid and as a player, and he especially understood why Coach Powers liked him. He played hard, ran the offense the way Coach wanted it run and hardly ever deviated. Even on fast breaks, he did something Coach Powers was always preaching: stopped at the foul line every time, passed to one cutter or the other, only shot the ball himself as a last resort.

He was just the wrong partner for Rasheed.

Danny never said it out loud, even to the other guys, mostly because he knew he wasn't playing well enough himself to be talking about anybody else. But Cole had no feel for the game. He had no imagination. Cole had tunnel vision. He could only see the offense or the defense they were supposed to be running. Like he was some kind of RoboGuard. He didn't know when it was time to forget about the play, just give the ball to Rasheed no matter what they were trying to run.

Danny did.

Danny and Rasheed were both point guards, but that never seemed to matter. When they got the chance, they worked together the way Danny and Ty had with the Warriors.

If you looked at them, you might think they couldn't be more different, and they couldn't have come from more different backgrounds.

But Rasheed had been right: They played the same game.

And in a camp full of big guys, Danny was convinced that the Celtics were at their best when they went small. That meant either Ben Coltrane or David Upshaw at center, Danny and Rasheed at guard, Tarik at power forward and Will at small forward. If Danny were the coach here the way he had been in travel—yeah, right, another in-your-dreams, Walker—those would be the five guys on the court when they were trying to win the game. Make the other team match up with their speed and shooting and ability to push the ball.

Which is what they were doing now against Ty's team, the Cavs, at the end of the first half.

The game was originally scheduled on one of the outside courts, but the refs for their game had ended up someplace else. So it was being played in The House after the regular four o'clock game in there, and there were a ton of kids in the stands, even though it was getting close to dinnertime.

Danny thought, *It's the same with everybody*. If there was a game going on, you stopped to watch it. You couldn't help yourself.

Jack Arnold and Ty had scored most of the points for their team. Rasheed was carrying the Celtics, doing it today by scoring and rebounding. The Celtics were up four points with the ball, holding it for the last shot of the half. Danny had been in the backcourt with Rasheed for the past five minutes or so, playing at the Indy 500 speed that Coach Rossi and the Cavs always liked to play.

They had been in a time-out when Coach Powers told Danny to go into the game. He looked at Danny and Rasheed, pointed one of those bony fingers at them and said, "I want you to find a way to slow this game down."

Rasheed just shook his head.

"Coach, we can try," he said. "But it would be like trying to ride a bike in the fast lane. We can beat these guys at their own game."

"You're sure?"

"Yeah," Rasheed said, in that confident way he had. "I'm sure."

Now they were down to the last play of the half. The play Coach

Powers had called from the sideline was simple enough: "Spread." It was one you saw the real Cavaliers use all the time for LeBron James, at the end of a quarter or half or game.

Give him the ball, give him some room, tell him to make something happen.

On their team it meant giving the ball to Rasheed a few feet inside the half-court line and giving him so much room it looked like he and his man were playing one-on-one.

Jack Arnold, the Boston kid, was guarding him. But Danny could see Ty hanging off Tarik, his man, ready to cut Rasheed off if he tried to go all the way to the basket when he finally made his move. Danny was on the right wing, knowing he was nothing more than a place for Rasheed to dump the ball off if he got jammed up on his drive.

Will, who'd made a couple of threes earlier, was on the other wing, just to give the defense something else to think about.

With fifteen seconds to go, Rasheed took the ball off his hip. He was always saying that it drove him crazy watching the NBA, he always thought guys waited too long to make their move. He started his now. Left-hand dribble, then right. Then left and right again. Two lightning crossovers that did exactly what they were supposed to: staple-gun Jack's feet to the floor.

He was past Jack then.

Ty came up on his right, the Cavs' center took away any room he had on his left. When the center moved up, Will's man dropped down to guard Ben Coltrane.

Nowhere for Rasheed to go. He gave a quick look at the clock and then, to the surprise of everybody in the place, Danny included, he wheeled and put the ball over his head and fired a screaming two-hand pass to Danny.

Kicking it over to him the way he had that first time they'd really played together in the backcourt, the day Danny had shot the air ball instead of passing it back to him.

He was wide open, about twenty feet from the basket, having pinched in. Ty ran right at him, waving his arms, thinking Danny had to be shooting.

But Danny wasn't shooting, and not just because he couldn't even see the basket over Ty's long skinny arms.

He wasn't shooting because of this:

He wasn't making the same mistake twice on a last shot.

This time he was getting the ball back to Rasheed.

The clock above the basket said five seconds.

There was no way to get the ball over Ty, and way too much traffic on either side of Ty to try a bounce pass around him.

Only one opening Danny could see:

Between Ty's legs.

Danny put the ball on the floor and rolled it along the floor, rolled it through his legs as hard as he could, before Ty had a chance to react.

All Rasheed, wide open himself now, had to do was lean over and grab it, and he had a layup.

But he took his eye off the ball for a split second, like a baseball infielder taking his eyes off a routine ground ball. Rasheed was probably as shocked as everyone in the gym that a pass was coming to him this way.

The ball went through his hands as easily as it had gone through Ty and rolled out of bounds as the horn for the half sounded.

Rasheed banged an open palm against the side of his head in frustration, then looked at Danny and pointed to himself. Like, My bad. Danny just smiled. It would have been one heck of an assist.

When he turned from Rasheed, Coach Powers was already on him.

"What was that?" he said.

Not talking in his mean-quiet voice now, talking loud enough for people already in the mess hall to hear him.

He pointed the finger of death at Danny and said, "Did you think you were bowling? Are you ever going to learn?"

He's acting like I lost the game, Danny thought, *because of one stupid pass.*

Except it hadn't been stupid, that was the thing.

Nothing else was happening in The House. He could feel everybody just watching him and Coach.

"Are you *ever* going to learn?" Coach Powers repeated.

Danny just stood there with his head down, taking it again, good at taking it by now, when he heard the sound of the applause.

The guys in the stands were clapping because he was getting yelled at by his coach?

But then Danny heard something else, something much more amazing than applause, heard a calm grown-up voice saying, "Hey, take it easy there, Ed." Heard the voice saying, "That looked like something I'd try, to tell you the truth."

Danny turned around, feeling himself smile as he did, somehow knowing who the voice belonged to before he even put a face with it.

Josh Cameron.

Josh Cameron himself: in a Rolling Stones T-shirt and cut-off jeans and unlaced green Nikes, a baseball cap turned backward on his head, shaking Danny's hand and saying, "Cool pass, kid."

THE PLAY-OFFS IN DANNY'S AGE GROUP STARTED THE WEDNESDAY OF the last week at Right Way. If you won your first two games, the final was scheduled for Saturday night in The House, in front of the whole camp, plus any parents who had showed up that day to pack their kids up and take them home. So it was a little like having championship weekend and parents' weekend all wrapped up into one huge deal.

Now all the Celtics had to do was make it to Saturday night.

They were talking about that at dinner the night before the play-offs. It was a weird feeling, the Middletown guys had decided, knowing that if the Celtics won, it meant Ty lost. If Ty's team, the Cavs, won the championship, it meant that Danny and Will lost.

"Or we could all lose," Tarik said. "Any of you bracketologists ever think of that?"

"Shut up," Will said. "That would mean Lamar wins."

"Not happenin'," Rasheed said.

Danny said to Ty and Will, "When was the last time we all weren't on the same side for a big game?"

"Biddy," Will said. "When we were all eight. Ty made that layup at the buzzer, remember?"

"Over me," Danny said. "Like I wasn't there."

"Shoulda done your flop thing," Rasheed said.

"Thing" came out "thang" with him sometimes.

"I don't flop," Danny said.

Tarik groaned. "Oh, sweet Lord, here we go again," he said.

"Nah," Rasheed said. "Now we're on the same side."

"Except for Ty," Will said.

"Remember, it's only summer ball," Ty said.

"I know," Danny said. "It just feels like more now."

He had played a lot the last two games of the regular season, after they'd finally beaten the Cavs the day of his famous bowling-ball pass. Ever since then, Coach Powers had coached as if Josh Cameron were looking over his shoulder, especially in the second half of the Cavs game, when Danny had gotten to play the point as much as Rasheed, dished out a bunch of assists, played pretty much his best all-around game in Maine, maybe even fooled Josh Cameron into thinking this was the way he always played for Coach Powers.

When the game had ended, Danny actually felt good about things for a change, felt some of his old confidence coming back. Josh had come back over to him and said, "You're Richie Walker's boy, right?"

Danny said, yes sir, that was him, all right.

"I should've figured that out the minute you made that pass," Josh said. Then he clapped Danny on the back and yelled over to Coach Powers, "Hey, Ed, I've got my eye on this guy."

Coach Powers pointed at Josh and nodded, like the two of them were in perfect agreement.

When they were outside that day, Tarik had said to Danny, "Well, looky there. Coach Ed seems to have swallowed up his own bad self all of a sudden."

"For now."

"Know what that old man's problem is?" Tarik said. "He just plain forgot what he loved about this game in the first place."

Maybe it was a coincidence, maybe not, but their last two games, Danny had played as much with the first unit as Cole had. Sometimes more. A week ago, he couldn't wait to get out of here. Now he couldn't wait for the play-offs to start.

Summer ball.

Only more.

Danny talked to his mom that night on the telephone. He was hoping to talk to both his parents, mostly because he hadn't talked to his dad one time since the night he'd told him about faking the injury. But his mom informed him that his dad was out taking his nightly walk.

"My dad?" Danny said. "Walking for, like, *exercise*?"

"He says that if he's going to coach next season, he's not doing it from a folding chair."

"Mom," Danny said, "you sure he's not there and just doesn't want to talk to me?"

"He's calmed down about the whole knee thing," she said, then quickly added, "Somewhat, anyway. You know your dad. He just needs longer to work through things than most people."

Danny said, "Is he coming with you when you come to pick me up?"

When she didn't answer right away, Danny knew.

"It's a long time for him to sit in the car," his mom said.

"The finals are on Saturday night if we make it."

There was a pause and then his mom said, "I know. And now let's change the subject, shall we?"

"Fine with me."

Ali Walker said, "So, how goes the battle?"

"Still a battle," Danny said, then filled her in on his fight with Lamar, his suspension, Tess's camera. How he and Rasheed were boys now. Josh Cameron giving him a shout-out after he made the funky pass. When Danny was done, he felt like he'd just made some kind of presentation in front of her class: "How I Spent My Summer Vacation," by Danny Walker.

"I'm sorry about the fight, Mom," he said. "But he was picking on Zach."

His mom surprised him then. The way she surprised him a lot. "Don't beat yourself up because a big guy was about to beat up a little guy."

"I told you I wouldn't fight."

"And I told you," she said, "that one of the secrets to life is *picking* your fights."

"Play-offs start tomorrow," he said.

"How's the old coach?"

"Same old. But he's been letting me play more."

"*Hel*-lo," his mom said. "He wants to win, right?"

Danny smiled. "Thanks, Mom."

"You don't need more of a pep talk?" she said. "I've got a lot more material."

"I'm good."

"Yes, you are," she said. "You are the goodest."

Danny said, "And you're an English teacher?"

"See you Saturday night for the big game," she said.

"If we make it that far."

"You will."

"You're sure of that?"

"It's who you are, kiddo," she said.

"Do me a favor?"

"Anything."

"Remind Dad of that if you get a chance."

The Celtics, as the number 6 team, drew the Bulls, number 3, in the first round. If they beat the Bulls, that meant they were probably going to play the Cavs, Ty's team, in the semis.

Then, if everything worked out the way it was supposed to, they'd play the Lakers, the top seed, in the finals.

Them against Lamar.

Sometimes you didn't get to pick your fights.

Sometimes, Danny thought, *they picked you.*

"Winning the championship, that's what you came here for," Coach Powers said in their pregame huddle.

Danny wanted to say, No, that's what *you* came here for.

They had split their two games with the Bulls, basically a two-man team with the two Brooklyn AAU guys, Kareem Dell and TJ Tucker. The Celtics had lost the first one when Danny shot the air ball at the end, then won the last regular-season game, one Rasheed said didn't count because the Bulls' coach, Coach Pedulla, had barely played Kareem or TJ in the second half.

"Understand," Rasheed had said to Danny in the layup line. "They didn't *want* to win yesterday. They wanted the seedings the way they already were, them at three and us at six. You hear what I'm tellin' you? These guys wanted us."

"My mom always says, be careful what you wish for," Danny said, grinning at him.

"Mine, too."

Cole started with Rasheed in the backcourt. Danny figured the way Coach Powers had been using him, he'd get in at the end of the first quarter or maybe start the second. But when the Celtics got behind by ten points after the first three minutes, in a blink, Coach Powers said, "Walker."

Danny was a few seats down from him. "Yes, Coach?"

Coach Powers turned and said, "I was wondering if you might be interested in going into the game?"

Now Danny jumped up. "Yes, Coach!"

"Play the point for a little bit," he said, "and cover that pesky boy with the crew cut. See if we can get him to do the same with you at the other end."

The pesky boy with the crew cut, and more freckles than Danny had ever seen on one face, was Ricky Hartmann. By now, having gone through the regular season and seen a bunch of games, Danny knew Ricky was pretty much the one guy at Right Way you didn't want guarding you, under any circumstances. Will and Tarik, who had made it their mission to know as much as possible about as many campers as possible, said Ricky was a defensive back in football at home in Philadelphia. Before he would foul out of a game, and he fouled out of almost every game, he came after you like he was blitzing a quarterback, sometimes from the quarterback's blind side.

He took Danny now, the way Coach Powers wanted.

"Oh, man, is this ever taking one for the team," Danny said to Rasheed a couple minutes later, while Tarik took two foul shots. Ricky Hartmann had already fouled Danny once, sending him sliding into the first row of bleachers when the two of them dove for a loose ball.

"You're *part* of this team now," Rasheed said. "That's the main thing."

It wasn't as if Danny came into the game and started running rings around Ricky Hartmann. Ricky aggressively bodied up on him every chance he got, held him when the ref wasn't looking, even hip-checked Danny right off the court one time when Danny tried to get out on a fast break Rasheed was leading. Somehow, though, Danny held his own. More importantly, Rasheed, even with Kareem guarding *him* now, was getting some room to maneuver, starting to get his points in bunches.

The Celtics cut the lead to four by halftime.

It felt like a real game now.

Right before the second half started, Coach Powers said, "Same group we opened the game with." Then he paused. "Except for Cole. Walker, you take his place for now."

When they started to break the huddle, Danny felt somebody grab his arm, hard, from behind.

He turned around and saw that it was Cole.

"This should've been your spot all along," he said. "Now, go kick their butts."

There were no surprises from the Bulls, not in a play-off game. They were just going to ride Kareem and TJ as far as they could. With seven minutes left, the two of them had stretched the Bulls' lead to twelve points, their biggest lead of the game. The Bulls had gone to a zone, and Rasheed, playing with four fouls, wasn't just missing, he'd gotten frustrated trying to get open looks at the basket.

Finally Coach Powers, more out of desperation than anything else, called a time-out and put Will Stoddard in the game, said he was giving Will a chance to be what he called his designated zone-buster.

Even now, facing elimination in the first round, Will was incapable of being anybody except himself.

"You know what they say, Coach?" Will said.

"What do they say, Mr. Stoddard?"

Will hit him with one of his favorite lines then. "There's no greater tragedy in basketball than being hot and not knowing it."

"You think this is funny, son?" Coach Powers said.

"No, sir," Will said. "Just fun."

Will hit his first two threes. Then another shot with his foot on the three-point line. And all those baskets did was change everything for the Celtics, just like that. Danny had seen it before, a couple of baskets changing everything. Now it had happened here, against the Bulls. It was one of the things Danny loved about sports, how fast things changed. His dad always said that it was something that had always fascinated him about all sports, not just basketball—how fragile games could be, how they could turn on the smallest moment or play, and how you better be ready when they did.

Will had done exactly what he was supposed to do, which meant he had shot the Bulls right out of their zone. Ricky Hartmann was still on Danny when the Bulls went back to man-to-man, Kareem was still on Rasheed. With two minutes left, Rasheed beat Kareem off the dribble and seemed to have a clear path right down the middle. But Ricky Hartmann switched off Danny and got in his way just as Rasheed dropped his shoulder for his drive.

Rasheed went down, Ricky went down.

Ball went in.

Nick Pinto, reffing the game, didn't hesitate, signaling offensive foul.

Rasheed had fouled out.

Anybody else, Danny knew, including Danny himself, would have jumped up and protested the call, because it was that close. And usually a call like this, this late in the game, this late in an *important* game, went to star players.

Rasheed just sat there. Nick, answering a question Rasheed hadn't even asked, said, "He beat you to the spot."

Rasheed just shook his head, stayed where he was, arms folded across his knees. Chillin'. Even now.

Danny put a hand down to pull him up. Before Rasheed reached up to take it, he looked at Danny and said, "World's full of danged floppers, you know?"

"I thought it was on him this time," Danny said and pulled him up.

"Yo," Rasheed said. "Now you all got to pick me up in more ways than one."

Danny grinned at him. "Don't worry, dog," he said. "I got you."

Kareem chased down a loose ball with forty seconds left, turned around and made a truly outrageous three-pointer to put the Bulls ahead by one. Will missed a wide-open three at the other end, first shot he'd missed since Coach Powers put him in. As soon as TJ got the rebound, David Upshaw fouled him.

Twenty-two seconds left.

Coach Powers called their last time-out.

He said they were going small: Danny, Tarik, Will, Cole, plus David. Coach said that if TJ made both free throws, putting the Bulls up three, to look for Will at the other end, out beyond the arc.

If they only needed a two to tie or win the game, Coach Powers said for them to spread it once they got over half court.

"Spread it for who?" Danny said.

"You," Coach Ed Powers said.

"Got it," he said, like he always ended up with the rock with the game on the line.

TJ, who could do everything on a court except shoot free throws, missed them both. David Upshaw got the rebound, Danny pushed the ball hard over half-court then put the brakes on, passed it to Will and got it right back.

He put the ball on his hip and checked the clock.

Ricky Hartmann was eyeballing him, in a defensive crouch, looking as if he really might try to tackle Danny as soon as he made a move.

Danny started his dribble with ten seconds left. Ricky got right up on him. Danny dusted him with a crossover that was up there with Rasheed's best. Then he broke into the clear at the top of the circle.

TJ Tucker came over from the corner, covering about twenty feet with about two long strides.

It had come down to Danny against TJ again, the way it had when Danny shot the air ball.

TJ Tucker, whose arms were even longer than broom handles.

Danny slowed up just slightly at the free throw line, pulled the ball in, went into his shooting motion, hands in perfect position.

TJ, with those amazing ups of his, went *way* up, like he wasn't just trying to block the shot, like he wanted to be another guy catching one of Danny's shots.

Small problem.

Danny didn't shoot it.

He sold his fake, though, sold it as well as he'd ever sold a fake in his life.

Then he waited for gravity.

What goes up, he thought, must come down.

When TJ did come down, like he was falling out of the sky, Danny leaned in and waited for the contact he knew was coming, then right before TJ landed on top of him, he fired the ball at the basket.

He landed hard.

But rolled like a champ.

The way Nick Pinto said little guys had to.

Then Danny got up, tucked his jersey back into his shorts, went to the line, knocked down the two free throws that put the Celtics into the second round, the whole thing becoming official once Kareem missed a wild heave at the very end.

Danny was at half-court when the horn sounded. He felt a tap on his shoulder and turned around.

"Glad you hung around this place?" Nick Pinto said.

24

THEY WENT INTO CEDARVILLE AFTER THE GAME, NICK PINTO DRIV-ing. Even after everything that had happened at Right Way, it still seemed to Danny as if it were just the other day that Nick had driven them to camp from the Portland airport.

"Sure am going to miss that hooptie bus," Tarik said. "The 4 train doesn't shake like this when it comes into the Yankee Stadium stop."

Nick dropped them in front of Pops and they went right for their favorite booth, where everybody ordered milk shakes, except for Rasheed, who said the only way to celebrate was with a root beer float.

"Hooptie," Will said, shaking his head. "Another cool word."

"Maybe you should have been keeping a diary on stuff Tarik says," Danny said. "In case you forget some of them when you get home."

"Get home and deal with your general heartbreak on not being black," Tarik said.

Will had ripped through his milk shake, now made a loud suck-ing sound as he finished it. "You have to keep throwing that in my face," he said.

Ty wasn't with them—his coach had scheduled a nighttime

practice to get the Cavs ready to play the Celtics in the semis tomorrow night.

Will said, "We should have T-shirts made when we get home, saying, 'I Survived Basketball Camp.'"

"On the back you can put 'Barely,'" Danny said.

Tarik and Rasheed said they were going to walk down to the dock and buy some taffy. Will and Danny said they'd wait for them in front of Pops, on one of the benches near the front door.

Just the two of them for a change, not surrounded by the other campers at Right Way. *Now, this felt right,* Danny thought, felt like all the other times when it was just him and Will Stoddard.

"What?" Will said.

"I didn't say anything."

"But you want to," Will said. "You forget sometimes that I know you as well as Tess does."

There was a piece of paper near his sneakers, some kind of flyer somebody had dropped. Danny picked it up, crumpled it into a ball, tossed it into the wire basket near the curb without it even touching the sides.

"Money," he said.

"I'm good with that," Will said, grinning. "Because I am willing to pay you to find out what's bothering you all of a sudden."

"I've been thinking about something since the game ended," he said. "If we win, which means I win, that means Coach Powers wins, too."

"Only you want him to lose," Will said.

"Yeah," Danny said. "I want there to be some secret formula where we win and he loses."

"Because if we win the camp championship, he gets the only thing that matters to him," Will said, "even though he did everything possible to drag us down. Basically, it's like dealing with our parents. There are times when they know they're wrong about something and we know they're wrong, but they'd never admit that in a million trillion years."

"I want him to admit he was wrong about me," Danny said.

"First we win the game," Will said, "and then we worry about the rest of it."

"You do sound like Tess sometimes."

"I'm going to take that as a compliment," Will said, then gave him a sideways look. "She definitely can't hang around for the finals if we make it?"

"She's out of here tomorrow on JetBlue," Danny said. "Her mom wants her back."

"So we call her after the game and tell her all about it," Will said.

Danny looked at Will Stoddard, the best friend of his life, and said, "You think we're gonna win this game?"

Will reached out so Danny could bump him some fist.

"We always have," he said.

They beat the Cavs the next day, beat them by six points finally, beat them because of what became a one-on-one game between Rasheed and Ty, and Rasheed was better on this day. Maybe it would have been different the next day. But today is the only one that ever matters in sports.

It wasn't that either one of them was hogging the ball or being selfish, because neither was that kind of player. They hadn't suddenly morphed into being Lamar. It was just that Rasheed finally took over for the Celtics, and Ty took over for the Cavs, and the two of them guarding each other and getting after each other was the way this game was supposed to end. It was like an old-time play-off game that Richie Walker had taped for Danny off ESPN Classic once: Larry Bird and the Celtics went up against Dominique Wilkens and the Atlanta Hawks, matching each other basket for basket, until Wilkens started missing at the end and the Celtics won.

Even the coaches seemed to get what was happening. Maybe that was why Coach Powers finally let Rasheed guard Ty and Coach Tom Rossi put Ty on Rasheed at the other end and then both coaches pretty much stayed out of the way after that.

Rasheed scored the last ten points for the Celtics. Ty was on his way to doing pretty much the same thing until he missed a couple of open jumpers. Danny knew why, even if nobody else in the gym did, knew what happened to Ty's shot when his legs got tired. He stopped elevating enough, started firing line drives at the basket.

Ty even missed the front end of a one-and-one with forty seconds to go. After that, Rasheed made six straight free throws and the Celtics were in the finals against the Lakers, who had blown out the Knicks, biggest blowout of the whole camp, somebody said, in the first semifinal game.

When the Celtics–Cavs game was over, Rasheed went and found Ty at half-court, gave him what Tarik called the "brother snap." They shook hands by locking their thumbs, pulled close together and bumped shoulders, backed away, shook hands again with the tips of their fingers, snapped their hands away to finish.

Then Danny heard Ty say, "You were better."

Rasheed said, "Nah, I just had more legs than you at the end."

"You're the best I've ever played against," Ty said.

"Today," Rasheed said. He knew. It was always about today. "Next time it would probably be you."

"Hope there is one," Ty said. "A next time, I mean."

They all heard Lamar then.

"Don't come to me looking for a big hug when we whup y'all's butts in the finals," he said in a loud voice. Everybody in the gym looked at him now.

Which, Danny knew, was the point.

Rasheed just calmly stared at him, without saying a word. Stared for what felt to Danny like five minutes. You could see how uncomfortable it made Lamar.

"Got nothin' to say, 'Sheed?" Lamar said.

Rasheed just shrugged.

Lamar stood there, nervous now, cracking his knuckles, the scene not playing out the way he intended. "Well, we'll see what you got to say Saturday night. You and your little boy there."

Now Rasheed smiled.

And Lamar gave up.

"That's right, give me that big spit-eating grin now," he said. "Till I wipe it right off your face on Saturday."

He walked out of The House.

Danny said to Rasheed, "That was the coolest trash talk of all time."

"I didn't say anything," Rasheed said.

"That's why," Danny said.

On Friday night they watched Zach's team win the eleven- and twelve-year-old championship, win it so easily Zach didn't even have to play the last five minutes of the game.

He was the smallest kid on either team, and it didn't matter. If you knew anything about basketball—and maybe even if you didn't—he was the only player on either team you were interested in watching. Mostly because he was playing a different game than the rest of the kids, even the ones who were a lot bigger than he was.

It was as if he knew something the rest of them, even his own teammates, didn't.

When the game was over, before the trophy presentation, Danny saw an ending to this kind of game he had seen before, watched a couple of the bigger kids put Zach up on their shoulders and carry him around like he was the trophy.

Danny waited until the celebration was over before he went over to Zach, carrying the bag with the gift inside.

He handed it to Zach now, and Zach opened it up to find the same indoor/outdoor ball Lamar had wrecked on him. Danny had spotted it in the window at Bob's Sports in Cedarville.

"You didn't have to get me anything," Zach said. "I'm the one who should be getting you something."

"You were great tonight," Danny said. "Awesome, dude. I mean it."

Zach looked down. "I wouldn't have made it without you," he said.

"Yeah," Danny said, "you would have. My father always tells me something about sports." It was amazing how many times he quoted his dad. Even now, when his dad wasn't speaking to him. "He says that the guys who aren't any good, they're the ones who always find excuses. But the guys who *are* good enough, they always find a way. It just took you a little time to find your way here."

Then Danny said he'd see Zach back at Gampel later, there was something he needed to do right now.

Go someplace and play.

Danny cut across the lawn and made his way to the bad court. The lighting on it was as bad as the playing surface—the best light actually came from the end nearest the parking lot, where there were a couple of old-fashioned-type streetlamps.

Danny had picked up a ball along the way, one lying near the court outside Staples. And had stopped in the mess hall to get a folding chair. Something to use as a target for his passes, just like in his driveway.

So he had a ball and a chair and a court all to himself. When it was like that, there really was no such thing as a bad court.

He went through all his stuff now. Dribbled the length of the court with his right hand, came back with his left, then up and down again, this time switching hands as he went.

Free throws, outside shots, driving layups with both hands.

Hitting the chair with two-hand chest passes, then bounce passes, even a couple of no-looks, knocking the chair over and picking it up and then hitting it again.

Then he started moving the chair around. Drive and pass to one corner, then the other. Move it out to the wing and hit it there.

Getting ready for the game the only way he knew how.

He started driving hard to the basket, pulling up, shooting his high-arc shot over an imaginary tall guy, Danny imagining arms that stretched to the stars. He kept taking that shot until he could make it three times in a row.

It was late now, and he should have been tired, but he wasn't, even working himself like this. Mostly because this wasn't work, not to him.

He didn't know how much he'd get to play against the Lakers. Coach Powers had talked a lot at practice today about how big the Lakers were, even in the backcourt. But Danny knew this: He was going to be ready, no matter how little his name got called. His mom was going to be there tomorrow. He was *not* going to stink up the joint in front of her.

Or Josh Cameron.

When he finally stopped, out of breath, sweating, he felt like he'd just finished playing a game.

It was then that he turned and saw Coach Powers standing over near the woods, at the start of the path that took you back to the coaches' cabins.

Standing there like some kind of ghost.

Danny wanted to say something, call out to him. But there was nothing left to say. Nothing he could say at this point that was going to change anything between them.

So Danny just stood there, in what felt like the most natural pose in the world to him, ball on his right hip. Coach Powers stayed where he was, hands in his pockets. There was just the night between them.

Then he turned and walked into the woods. If Danny hadn't heard his slow steps on the gravel path he would have wondered if he really had seen a ghost, would have wondered if the coach had even been there at all.

THERE WAS SOMEONE WITH ALI WALKER WHEN DANNY FINALLY SPOT-
ted her Saturday morning in the crowd of parents walking up from
the parking lots.

It wasn't his dad.

Just the next best thing on this particular day.

Tess.

Camera bag slung over her shoulder.

After Danny had broken loose from his mom, after a Mom hug
that tried to squeeze all the oxygen out of his body, Danny said to
Tess, "You're supposed to be home."

"Change of plans," she said. "It turns out that I'm hitching a
ride back with you guys."

It had been arranged when they'd gone off to camp that Ali
Walker was the designated parent from Middletown and would
drive Danny, Will and Ty home. Ali had brought her Suburban, so
there was plenty of room for Tess.

"So you get to see the big game," Danny said.

"I guess," Tess said, smiling at him. "I mean, as long as I'm
here."

Ali didn't want to talk about the big game, she wanted to tell
him that he needed a haircut as soon as he got home and was he
packed and if he was packed, was he sure he had everything?

Danny said yes, to all of the above. She said, prove it, so he and his mom and Tess walked down to Gampel.

Zach was sitting on his bunk when they got there, his parents having left a message that they were stuck in traffic somewhere on the highway between Boston and here.

Ali said, "Is this the budding superstar I've been hearing about?"

Zach stood, looked up, shook her hand and said, "Nice to meet you, Mrs. Walker."

They all stayed in Gampel while Danny proved to his mom that he hadn't forgotten anything major, and then they all went outside so Tess could take some pictures before lunch.

The game wasn't until seven-thirty, which meant there were still almost eight hours to wait. But Danny was fine with that. It was a great feeling, the sense of anticipation and the nervousness you got before a big game, as long as the day of the big game had finally arrived.

The only thing better was actually playing the game.

That never changed, no matter where the game was, no matter who it was against.

Even at camp.

There was a barbecue for the campers and parents that began a little after four o'clock. Things were set up that way so the players from both the Celtics and Lakers would have time to not only get something in their stomachs but actually digest it before the opening tip. It was at the barbecue, after Ali Walker and Danny and Tess had taken a quick trip into town so she could see Cedarville, that she finally got to meet Tarik and Rasheed.

"My son tells me you're even better than he thought you were in North Carolina," Ali said.

Rasheed grinned. "He means how good he thought I was until he flopped on me."

"I didn't flop," Danny said.

Ali said to Rasheed, "You're both probably talking to the wrong parent on this."

Danny looked at her. "How's Dad doing?" It was the first time they'd talked about him all day.

"I'm under strict orders to call him the minute the game is over."

When they sat down to eat, his mom was between Will and Tarik, which meant she spent the whole barbecue laughing her head off. It was funny, Danny thought now, watching her, seeing her as comfortable as she'd always been with his friends. Sometimes you didn't even know what you were missing when you were away from somebody until you were back with them. And one of the things he had missed most being up here at camp was the loud, happy sound of his mother's laughter.

He still wished his dad were here, for a lot of reasons, one of them being that this reminded him of all the other games his father had missed when his parents had been apart all those years, all those years when Danny had pretty much convinced himself that his dad was never coming back.

It also brought him back to the start of camp when he felt lower than dirt.

He looked up then, all the way across the mess hall, like this was some kind of weird cue, and saw Lamar Parrish, already dressed for the game in his Lakers jersey, glaring at him.

Lamar pointed to himself first, mouthed the word *Me,* then pointed at Danny.

You.

Danny turned and said to Will and Tarik and Rasheed, "You guys wanna go shoot?"

His mom said, "You hardly ate anything, not that a person would consider that any kind of breaking news."

"Mom," Danny said, "I can't sit here anymore, I gotta move."

She smiled at him and said, "Like a streak of light."

All Danny heard from Tess was the click of her camera.

Danny thought there was an outside shot that he might start, but Coach Powers went with their normal starting five, which meant Cole was with Rasheed.

Before they went inside The House to warm up, a few minutes after seven o'clock, Coach Powers took them all over to the lake side of the building, and sat them down in the grass. There were no locker rooms at The House, just bathrooms, so all pregame meetings like this always took place out here. It was a perfect night, not too hot, not too muggy.

The Celtics were stretched out in one long line. Coach Powers got down on one knee, so he was facing all of them.

"You get only so many games in your life when you play for a championship," he began. "I read in a book one time, I forget where, the writer asked, If there were only three or four sunsets you were going to see in your whole life, how valuable would they be? So if I told you that tonight was only one of the three or four times in your life when you might play for the title of something, how dear would you hold this one game of basketball?"

There was something in his eyes now Danny hadn't seen before, a light in them, some kind of spark.

Without looking around at his teammates, Danny knew the coach had their attention.

"It doesn't matter where the game is, or who it's against," he said. "But you know the feeling inside you is different today. You know because that feeling has been inside you since you got up this morning." He paused. "Because today *is* different, that's why. Today is different because you're playing for something today. Not a trophy. Or to prove something to me or the parents who are here or the counselors or the other coaches, or even Mr. Josh Cameron himself. You're here to prove something to yourselves tonight— that you're the best of the best."

He paused again and said, "People who don't play sports will never have this feeling for one day in their lives."

He's right, Danny thought. He hated to admit it, especially about a guy he'd hated from the first day. But Coach Powers was right. For the first time, Danny at least could see why he might have been a great coach in the first place.

"Every pass, every shot," he said, once more in that voice of his that made you strain to hear, pointing his finger at them. "Play every play as if the whole game is riding on it. From the time you step on that court in a few minutes, you keep one picture in your heads: You picture what the faces of the other team will look like if they beat you. *And then you do whatever it takes to make sure they don't.*"

Now Coach Powers was standing up, raising his voice at the same time, like he was giving a sermon in church.

"Are you going to let them beat you?"

"No!" they yelled back at him.

"Are we going to win the game?"

"Yes!"

"Then let's do this!"

They ran back inside.

They got back into layup lines for a couple of minutes, then shot around until the horn sounded. Will always waited until everybody else on the team was finished shooting and then stayed out until he made one more three. Danny always waited with him, and did now. So they were the last two back to the Celtics' huddle, Will a few feet ahead of him.

Before they got there, Danny got popped from his blind side like you did when somebody on your team didn't call out a pick in time.

He should have known who it was.

"Sorry," Lamar Parrish said to him. "You're so little I didn't see you."

For the whole first quarter, neither team was more than a basket ahead. Lamar was taking most of the shots for his team, Rasheed was doing the thing he did best for the Celtics, letting the game come to him, doing everything he could to get everybody else on his team involved. They had come out in a man-to-man, Coach Powers putting Rasheed on Lamar. The Lakers were in a zone because they were always in a zone, because as talented as Lamar was, there was no place you could hide him in a man-to-man—he was that lazy when the other team had the ball.

He didn't care about defense the way he didn't care about anything except shooting.

And himself.

The Lakers scored three quick baskets to start the second quarter, extending their lead to eight. That was when Danny got into the game. It did more to hurt the Celtics than help them. The other Laker guard, a redheaded kid named Tommy Main, was as tall as Lamar and impossible for Danny to guard. With Lamar taking a rest—because nobody at Right Way, not even him, was allowed to play all four quarters, not even in the play-offs—Tommy Main started posting Danny up almost every time the Lakers had the ball.

By the time Coach Powers realized what he was watching and put the Celtics into a zone, the Lakers were ahead by fourteen points.

With two minutes to go before the half, Coach Powers got Danny out of there. As Danny went past him to take a seat at the end of the bench, Coach snapped, "In a championship game, defense wins."

The Laker lead was still fourteen at the half. Coach Powers hustled them back outside, sat them down and immediately laced into the whole team, his voice a raspy whisper somebody even twenty feet away wouldn't have been able to hear.

This was *his* kind of trash talk, that voice you had to strain to hear, those blue-looking veins trying to pop right out of his forehead.

"I thought you wanted this as much as I do," he said. "I thought winning a championship still mattered in sports, as long as it was the championship of something. But apparently I was wrong. You're all playing like a bunch of quitters."

They all just sat there, some of them with their heads down, just taking it from him. He didn't allow for one second that the Lakers might just be playing better, that the Lakers might want to win the game, too. As usual, Coach Powers was putting it all on them, calling them the worst thing in the world:

Quitters.

What Richie had called Danny.

All Danny could think of was getting back inside, doing whatever he could do to help his team win, and then leaving this one gym knowing that this guy was never going to be his coach ever again.

He would try to win the game for himself and for his team-

230

mates, and then he was gone. In the language of Tarik Meminger, he was taillights.

"Am I making myself clear, Mr. Walker?"

Danny knew he'd missed something. He just didn't know *what* he had missed, the way it was in class when your mind wandered and then you realized the teacher was talking to you. So he just said, "Yes sir."

Coach Powers said, "For the rest of this game, if you don't guard, you don't play."

He was standing over Danny now.

"But between you and I," Coach Powers said, "you haven't guarded anybody yet, have you?"

Danny heard his mom before he saw her.

"Between you and me," Ali Walker said.

Coach Powers turned around. Danny's mom was standing right there, a bottle of water in her hand, Tess at her side.

"I beg your pardon," Coach Powers said.

"It's not between you and I," Ali said. "It's between you and me." She was smiling pleasantly, but Danny knew the look, it was the same as if she was hitting him right in the teeth.

"And you are?"

"Ali Walker."

"Oh," Coach Ed Powers said. "Mr. Walker's mother."

"Danny's mom," she said. "Richie's wife. I'm sure you remember my husband."

There was something about her body language, the way she was looking at him, that smile fixed in place, that let Coach Powers know he shouldn't tangle with her, not here. "I'm not too good with words sometimes," he said.

She said, "So I'm told," and walked away.

Coach Powers took a couple of steps away from his players,

as if he wanted to say one more thing to her, but didn't. Tarik took the opportunity to whisper in Danny's ear, "Oh, baby. Your mom . . . from *downtown!*"

Coach Powers came back to them now, trying to act as if nothing had happened. He talked about what they were going to do on defense and offense to start the second half. All the while Danny kept thinking, *However much I thought I was buried before with this coach, this time they're going to need heavy equipment to dig me out.*

As they started back toward the gym, Coach Powers caught up with Danny, stopped him with a tap on his shoulder.

"Between you and *me?*" he said. "I meant what I said before."

"I know you did, Coach."

"You don't guard, you don't play, whether your mother likes me or not."

Danny stopped at the outdoor fountain for a drink of water, splashed some water on his face, trying to get himself fired back up after everything that had just happened.

He didn't need to worry about that.

When he walked back inside, the first person he saw, just inside the door, was his dad.

26

HIS DAD LOOKED THE SAME AS ALWAYS: PLAIN GRAY T-SHIRT, JEANS, unlaced Reebok high-tops. He needed a haircut. From a distance, anybody who didn't know him could have confused him with one of the counselors.

But there wasn't much distance between Danny and his dad for long. He ran right for Richie Walker and hugged him, not caring whether his teammates were watching or not.

"You came," he said.

"I would've been here for the start of the game, but JetBlue picked this day to have equipment problems at JFK," his dad said.

"You're here now. That's all I care about."

His dad pushed back, looked down at him. "I'm always telling you that you gotta let stuff go eventually. So I followed my own advice for a change. I was sitting there at the breakfast table this morning, thinking about you and your mom being here and me being there by myself . . ." He grinned at Danny and shrugged, looking even more like a kid.

Danny pointed to the scoreboard. "You haven't missed much."

"Can you beat these guys?"

"I honestly don't know."

"Wrong answer," Richie Walker said, but he wasn't looking at Danny now. He was looking over him and past him, in the direction of the court.

"Hello, Ed," he said.

Danny turned. There was Coach Powers, standing a few feet away from them with his arms crossed.

"Richie," the coach said. "Long time no see."

Neither one of them made any kind of move to get closer, maybe shake hands. Danny just stood there, feeling as if he were between them now in more ways than one.

Finally Coach Powers said, "I'm sorry to break up this re-union, but we've got a game we're trying to win here," and started walking in that slow, straight-backed walk of his toward the Celtics' bench.

Richie Walker squeezed his son's shoulder.

"So go do that," he said. "Go win the game."

"He might only play me for, like, a couple more minutes."

"If he does," his dad said, "then make them the best couple minutes of your life."

Rasheed kept them in the game in the third quarter, getting in-side the Lakers' zone just enough, drawing the guys on the Lakers to him who actually wanted to play defense before he'd get another shot or feed David or Ben or Alex. And Tarik was doing a decent job on Lamar, bumping him every chance he got, whether Lamar had the ball or not, even getting Lamar to retaliate a couple of times and get called for fouls.

Still, the best the Celtics could do was trade baskets, and it was getting too late in the game for that. They were still too far behind.

Coach Ed wouldn't change his defense, though, wouldn't double Lamar or go to a zone. His way, to the end. The Coach Ed Powers My-Way-or-the-Highway Basketball Camp. Every once in a while, he would allow the Celtics to press for a couple of posses-sions. But as soon as Lamar or somebody got an easy bucket, he'd take the press off.

And through it all, Danny Walker was dying. Because he was just sitting there, feeling more like a cheerleader again than part of the team, trying to remember a time in his life when he couldn't get off the bench in the second half of a game like this.

Only he couldn't.

Maybe Coach Powers planned on sticking it to the whole family this time.

At the end of the third quarter, the Celtics were still down nine points, 47–38.

In the huddle Coach Powers said, "Now, listen up."

Rasheed Hill said, "No. *You* listen up."

Not raising his voice even a little bit. Just talking to Ed Powers the way he had always talked to them.

Rasheed pointed to Danny and said, "Put him in the game. Or take me out."

The only change of expression from the old man, Danny saw, was that big vein on his forehead.

"You're a great player, son," he said to Rasheed. "And I need you. But this is still my team."

"Play both of us or neither one of us," Rasheed said, standing his ground. "You got to declare now whether you want to win as much as you say." Rasheed looked at Danny. "How would you play these guys?"

Danny looked at Rasheed so he didn't have to look at Coach Powers, swallowed hard, then did something he'd wanted to do since the first day of practice:

Pretended Ed Powers wasn't even there.

Behind them he heard the buzzer from the scorer's table that meant the quarter break was over.

"Box-and-one," Danny said. "Me on Lamar, just to make him mad. Extend the help I get, and I'll need a lot, all the way to the

235

three-point line. And press every chance we get, our zone press, except with me still on Lamar."

Nick Pinto, reffing the final, tapped Powers on his shoulder. "Coach, I need your guys to get out there."

Coach Powers nodded. He looked older than ever, sad and old. His eyes were on Rasheed when he said, "Walker, get in for Tarik." Then he went and sat down.

"Yesssss!" Will hissed in Danny's ear.

It was Celtics' ball to start the fourth. Danny and Rasheed went to take it out. Danny allowed himself one quick look at his dad, who put his right hand down next to his knee and made it into a fist.

Danny said to Rasheed, "What just happened back there?"

Rasheed, his face as much a blank wall as ever, said, "I thought I told you I didn't come here to lose."

He took the ball out, Danny brought it up, head-faked Lamar at the top of their zone, got past him as easily as if he were walking through his own front door, no-looked a bullet pass to Rasheed on the right wing.

Rasheed for three.

Game on.

Lamar reacted to Danny guarding him pretty much the way Danny expected him to.

"Shoo, fly," he said.

But right away you could see how much it annoyed him. When Lamar didn't have the ball, Danny shadowed him wherever he went, getting in his space, bumping him the way Tarik had.

Turning the tables, finally.

Getting under *his* skin now.

Every chance Danny got, he would put a hand on him, the way

guys did all the time on defense, trying to keep their man located. As soon as he would, Lamar would say, "Get offa me!"

Danny didn't say a word back to him, didn't react even when Lamar would wait until he thought the refs weren't watching and slap his hand away. Or just give him a shove. It was like tetherball. Danny just kept coming back.

With five minutes left to play and the ball on the other side of the court, Danny was the one who gave Lamar a little shove. This time Lamar slapped his hand away so hard you could hear it all over the House.

Nick Pinto, who happened to be looking right at them, immediately whistled him for a technical.

"He hit me first, man, are you blind?" Lamar said.

Nick, already walking with Rasheed toward the free throw line, stopped. "I didn't quite catch that?"

"Yo," Lamar said. "He's got his hand on me all the time and doesn't get a whistle on that, is all I'm sayin'."

"You play, Lamar. I'll ref. Let's see if we can make that work for both of us."

Rasheed made two free throws on the technical. Celtics ball, side out. Danny threw a bounce pass to a cutting Rasheed for an easy layup.

And just like that, the Lakers' lead was down to two.

Lamar, steaming now, came out of the time-out their coach called and made a three. "See that right there, midget?" he said to Danny as he held his pose. "That right there is a man shot."

With a minute and a half left, the Celtics were still down a basket. Tarik got another rebound and Danny did a run-out, trying to beat the Lakers down the court, Tarik threw him a perfect pass at halfcourt.

Danny was flying to the basket, ahead of the pack, when the lights went out.

Lamar had actually made a play on defense.

He had come from the other side of the court, come flying himself, blocked Danny's shot, knocked him right off the court and into one of the closed doors that opened into the front hall.

The lights hadn't actually gone all the way out.

It was like somebody had put them on dimmer.

Somehow Danny hit his head and his knee at the same time. Right away he took the kind of inventory you did when you got hurt and knew his right knee—the one he'd tried to use to get himself out of here—hurt much worse than his head.

He didn't even think about rubbing it.

Just rolled over and sat up, like the whole thing was no big deal.

The first people he saw over him, no big surprise, were his parents. Behind them, he saw Coach Powers, not over to see how Danny was doing but in Nick Pinto's face, yelling at him about a foul.

Ali Walker said, "You okay?"

"I'm good."

Richie Walker made a face and knelt down next to Danny. He had only spent his whole life taking hits like this. "You hit that knee hard."

"I'm good, Dad, really." Danny made himself pop right up like he was shooting out of a toaster, somehow fixing a smile on his face as he did, remembering a Will line as he did:

Nobody fakes sincerity better than I do.

He heard himself get a big ovation.

"You don't have to prove anything," his dad said.

"Yeah, Dad, I do," Danny said. "More than I ever have in my life."

Coach Powers was arguing for a flagrant foul, as it turned out. But Nick said, "Coach, I know he drilled him pretty good, but he was playing the ball. Two shots, that's it."

Now Coach Powers came over to Danny. "Are you okay to take these free throws? Because if you aren't, the other team can pick anybody off our bench to shoot them."

"I'm okay."

"We need these."

No kidding, Danny wanted to say.

"If you're hurting, I can take you out after you shoot them," Coach Powers said.

"You're not taking me out of this game." Danny walked away from him, went over to the line and took the ball from Nick.

Made both.

Celtics 60, Lakers 60.

They were tied for the first time since 2 all.

One minute left now. Lakers' ball. Lamar took a pass out on the wing, but rushed his shot, the ball banging off the back of the rim. The rebound came out to Tarik. He took a couple of dribbles, then spotted Rasheed at the other end cutting to the basket, hit him with a long pass. Layup.

Celtics by two.

Lamar took the inbounds pass, dribbled up the court, took a three over Danny right away. Didn't run any clock, didn't look to pass. Kobe to the end.

Drained a three.

Lakers by one.

Before Tarik inbounded the ball, he gave a quick look to Coach Powers, knowing they had two time-outs left. But the old man just made a sweeping motion with his hand like he was throwing a ball underhanded.

Push it, he was saying.

Tarik gave it to Danny. Danny pushed it. On his first dribble, he felt his knee buckle underneath him and nearly went down. But he stayed up, got past half-court, wanting them to clear out for Rasheed.

Rasheed looked him off with his eyes.

Somehow Danny knew what he wanted.

Rasheed was out at the three-point line, on Lamar's side of the court, open. Lamar started to cheat out there, probably thinking everybody was like him, that Rasheed was going to hoist up a three.

Rasheed yelled at Danny to pass him the ball.

Danny made a two-hand chest pass.

Or what would have been a two-hand chest pass if he'd released the ball.

Only he didn't.

Lamar bit on the fake, came running out at Rasheed just as Rasheed passed him going the other way. Now Danny threw it to Rasheed. Who pulled up and took the kind of midrange jumper the announcers always said was becoming a lost art in basketball, in the world of the three-point shot.

Wet.

The Celtics were ahead by one, twenty seconds left. Time-out Lakers.

As they walked toward the bench, Rasheed said, "I like it better, the end of these games, when we're on the same side." Then he slapped Danny such a vicious high-five Danny thought his shoulder was going to come loose.

"As opposed to you flopping and whatnot," Rasheed said.

"Didn't flop," Danny said.

In the huddle, Coach Powers spoke directly to the five in the game for the Celtics: Danny, Rasheed, Tarik, Will, Ben. He said, "There's a million theories about this game. Lord knows, by now I've heard 'em all. But as far as I'm concerned, they always start at the same place: by getting one stop."

When they were back on the court Rasheed said to Danny, "Our game to win."

"Ours, period."

When Danny got with Lamar, Lamar made sure the refs weren't looking and patted Danny on the top of the head. "Still sending out a boy to do a man's job," Lamar said.

Danny looked up at him, trying to do his best impression of Rasheed's stare.

The Lakers pushed the ball, got it to Lamar right away, who pulled up outside the three-point line, one more hero shot fired.

And missed.

This one caromed off the back rim even harder than the one before. There were all these bodies fighting for position under the basket. Danny saw the long arm of Ben Coltrane, their tallest guy, rise up above the pack. Ben, not able to get both hands on the ball, was just trying to swat it away, get it away from the basket somehow. Get it out of there.

It went right to Lamar.

Danny was the only one near him.

He looked down the court, at the clock over their basket. Ten seconds left now.

He remembered Lamar pointing to him in the mess hall.

You and me, he'd said.

Here they were.

Danny saw Lamar's eyes flash up to the clock above his own

basket. Lamar on his dribble now, right-hand dribble, no surprise there, he went right most of the time, only went left as a last resort.

But he crossed over on Danny, trying to cross him up, and went left now. Danny stayed with him. Had to be five seconds now. Danny was counting the time off in his head, keeping his eye on the ball, hands out in front of him, chest high, just like Ty had showed him that day on the bad court.

Lamar put on the brakes.

Now! Danny thought.

As Lamar stopped his dribble and started to transfer the ball to his right hand to go into his shot, Danny flicked his own right hand out.

In that moment, the ball out there in front of Lamar, they were finally the same size.

Danny slapped the ball away.

Slapped it away and grabbed it and dribbled away from Lamar Parrish. Then he heard the horn sound ending the championship game.

Celtics 64, Lakers 63.

His guys got to him first, Will and Tarik and Rasheed. And Ty Ross, out of the stands. They started to lift him up, but Danny pulled back, smiling and shaking his head. "Nah," he said, "that's for little guys."

"Boy plays too big for that," Rasheed said.

"He sure does," Josh Cameron said.

Josh Cameron was there with Ali and Richie Walker, looking as if *he* were the proud parent all of a sudden. "I thought it was a mismatch on that last play," he said. "It just turned out to be a mismatch the other way."

Usually it was Danny's mom who got to him first, but this time it was his dad, cutting in front of her on knees that suddenly seemed twenty years younger than they were, putting his arms around him, leaning down and saying, "It's always about how you get up," he said.

Then his mom put a Mom hug on him.

When she pulled back, Danny saw Zach Fox standing behind her.

"He took the ball from me, you took it from him," Zach said.

Danny asked Zach if he knew where Tess was, and Zach smiled and pointed to the other end of the court. There she was, over near the Lakers' bench, at the end of the bench where Lamar Parrish sat with his head in his hands. For a second, Danny thought she was going to take the last shot of the day.

She had her new camera out and started to point it at Lamar. Then she stopped herself, as if she somehow knew Danny was watching her.

As if he was in her head for once.

She turned then and smiled like she was the brightest light in the place and pointed the camera at Danny instead.

By now the Celtics were in a big, loud, happy circle at mid-court, waiting for the trophy presentation to begin, arms around each other, weaving back and forth the way NBA players did some-times during player introductions, chanting "Whoo whoo whoo."

Danny started walking across the court toward them.

Coach Powers was in his way.

Danny didn't even try to read the look on his face, or figure out whether basketball had finally made him happy or not. He didn't wait for him to say anything, the buttoned-up coach in his buttoned-up Right Way shirt.

There was something Danny wanted to say to him, though.

But first he took the game ball off his hip, put it down in front of him and executed a *killer* soccer kick, catching the ball just right, sending it flying out the open doors, trying to kick it all the way to Coffee Lake.

Or maybe Canada.

"I could play soccer if I wanted," Danny said. "But I'm a basketball player."

Then he walked past the coach to be with his team.

ABOUT THE AUTHOR

MIKE LUPICA writes novels for sports fans both young and old. His first two books for young readers, *Travel Team* and *Heat*, reached #1 on the *New York Times* Best Seller List. He is also the author of the *New York Times* best-selling *Miracle on 49th Street*.

Mr. Lupica is a nationally syndicated columnist for the New York *Daily News* and can be seen Sunday mornings on ESPN's *The Sports Reporters*. He lives in Connecticut with his wife and their four children.